KELLY'S HERO

"Saved by the Bell" titles include:

Mark-Paul Gosselaar: Ultimate Gold

Mario Lopez: High-Voltage Star

Behind the Scenes at "Saved by the Bell"

Beauty and Fitness with "Saved by the Bell"

Dustin Diamond: Teen Star

The "Saved by the Bell" Date Book

▲   ▼   ▲

Hot new fiction titles:

Zack Strikes Back

Bayside Madness

California Scheming

Girls' Night Out

Zack's Last Scam

Class Trip Chaos

That Old Zack Magic

Impeach Screech!

One Wild Weekend

Kelly's Hero

KELLY'S HERO

by Beth Cruise

Collier Books
Macmillan Publishing Company
New York

Maxwell Macmillan Canada
Toronto

Maxwell Macmillan International
New York Oxford Singapore Sydney

Text copyright © 1993 by Collier Books,
Macmillan Publishing Company

Collier Books   Maxwell Macmillan Canada, Inc.
Macmillan Publishing Company   1200 Eglinton Avenue East
866 Third Avenue   Suite 200
New York, NY 10022   Don Mills, Ontario M3C 3N1

Macmillan Publishing Company is part of the
Maxwell Communication Group of Companies.

First Collier Books edition 1993

Printed in the United States of America

10   9   8   7   6   5   4   3   2

Library of Congress Cataloging-in-Publication Data
Cruise, Beth.
Kelly's hero / by Beth Cruise.—1st Collier Books ed.
p.   cm.
Summary: When Kelly becomes the victim of her boss's
sexual harassment, she wonders if she should ask her
boyfriend Zack to help her.
ISBN 0-02-042769-7
[1. Sexual harassment—Fiction.] I. Title.
PZ7.C88827Ke   1993
[Fic]—dc20   93-8706

To all the "Saved by the Bell" heroes

Chapter 1

▲ ▼ ▲ ▼ ▲

Zack Morris groaned as he sank into his usual seat at his usual table at the Max, the Bayside High hangout. He rested his forehead against the Formica. "I'm beat," he told his friends. "It's rough going to school for fourteen days straight."

"What are you talking about, Zack?" Lisa Turtle asked. "It's Friday afternoon."

"Yeah, preppy," A. C. Slater said as he reached for a nacho. "We only went to school for five days straight. Even I can count that high."

"Oooh. You must have been studying hard," his girlfriend, Jessie Spano, teased. She and Slater were the Odd Couple of Bayside High. She was a brain and Slater was a jock, and they never let each other forget it.

"Was it really only five days?" Zack asked. "I could have sworn it was longer."

"What's your problem?" Lisa said. "You didn't have any papers or tests this week. And you didn't get called to Mr. Belding's office once. That's a first."

To the students of Bayside High, Zack was known as the Prankster. To Mr. Belding, the principal, he was the Menace. Zack had been called to his office so many times that Mr. Belding wanted to charge him rent.

"That's exactly what I'm talking about," Zack said, stealing a nacho from Slater. "I promised Kelly I'd behave myself this week. She still hasn't gotten over *last* week, when I put the microphone to the PA system in the girls' locker room after gym."

"I thought that stunt was great, preppy," Slater chortled. "I found out that Tamara Talbot craves my bod. She's a major babe." He saw Jessie shoot him a furious look and quickly added, "Uh, not that it meant anything to me, though. Who cares what Tamara Talbot thinks?"

"Right," Samuel "Screech" Powers piped up in his squeaky voice. He nodded, his frizzy curls flying. "Just because she won the Miss Avocado Queen title at the Palisades County Fair doesn't mean *she's* anybody special. I mean, come on. Everyone knows the pig judging was the best."

"Put a cork in it, Screech," Jessie said warningly.

"No, thank you, Jessie," Screech answered politely. "Too dry. But I *will* take a nacho."

"Kelly just wants what's best for you, Zack," Jessie told him. "Especially since you just had that major run-in with your dad."

"Tell me about it," Zack groaned. "He took away my cellular phone. I mean, I was just *curious* what the area code for Afghanistan was. I didn't expect the operator to connect me."

"You didn't have to talk to Fazal for an hour and a half," Jessie pointed out.

"It was in the spirit of international cooperation," Zack protested.

"Yeah, *right*," Slater said.

Zack sighed. "My father didn't buy it, either."

"Speaking of Kelly, where is she?" Lisa asked, twisting around.

"She went to a job interview," Zack explained.

"But what about her job at the Yogurt 4-U?" Jessie asked. "I know she isn't crazy about it, but she never said anything about quitting."

"She didn't," Zack explained, taking a sip of soda. "But she needs to make more money. She wants to take this acting seminar in L.A. with Jamie Dolan. She got bit by the acting bug when we took that class trip to New York."

"Jamie Dolan?" Lisa breathed. "He's *gorgeous*. Sign me up."

"Me, too," Jessie said dreamily. When Slater frowned at her, she said quickly, "Not that his opinion would mean anything to me. Who cares what Jamie Dolan thinks?" She grinned saucily at Slater.

"*I* do," Lisa said fervently. "I care about every thought that passes through that curly headed, gorgeous brain." Lisa was a pretty African-American girl who managed to balance an interest in medicine with a devotion to boys and shopping.

"Anyway," Zack continued, "she thought she'd try waitressing somewhere a couple of nights a week and maybe Saturdays. Just for a month or so. Besides, Kelly says that working at the mall is too much temptation. She keeps spending her paycheck before she makes it to the parking lot."

Lisa gave a horrified gasp. "Zack, there is no such thing as too much temptation where shopping is concerned!"

"So what's up for this weekend?" Jessie asked. "I finished my homework in study hall today, so I'm ready to play. How about a game of doubles, Zack? Me and Slater against you and Kelly."

"We'll cream you guys," Slater promised, flexing a muscle.

Zack made a face. "The public courts are so crowded on Saturdays. Last week, Kelly and I had to wait for forty-five minutes."

"Well, I'm hitting the beach," Lisa said. "Will

Cruikshank is teaching me how to bodysurf. It's a blast."

"Not when somebody lands on your head," Zack said, wincing. "Last Sunday was so crowded that I got creamed by a two-hundred-pound cannonball. I almost drowned. Then when I surfaced, a surfboard bonked me on the head."

Slater nodded solemnly. "So *that* explains it. I always thought the doctor dropped you on your head when you were born. All this time, it's been surfboards at the beach."

"How about volleyball?" Jessie suggested.

"Two weeks ago, I tripped over somebody's cooler and went flying into the sea grass," Zack said. "I still have a bruise."

"Gee, Zack, lighten up," Lisa said. "You're making southern California sound like a battle zone."

"I don't know, Lisa. I heard they're sending in combat photographers to Palisades Beach to do a layout for the Sunday paper," Zack said gloomily.

"Are you sure you're not the teensiest bit grumpy because things are tense at home?" Jessie asked sympathetically. She lived next door to Zack, and her mom and Mrs. Morris were close friends.

"What's going down, dude?" Slater asked. "Everything okay at home?"

"Everything's changing," Zack said. "That's the problem. My dad is completely stressed out.

And it isn't just because of my little phone call to Afghanistan. You guys know he's wanted to start his own software company for years. Lately, he's been working really hard to get it off the ground, and he's super close. He's finally got a big backer on the line. This is a dream come true for him. I just hope he doesn't crack from the pressure."

"It sounds pretty rough," Lisa said sympathetically.

Zack nodded. "Yeah. We're hanging in. But I still won't take back anything I said about Palisades Beach. The place is a zoo on weekends."

"Speaking of zoos," Screech said. "That brings me to what I want to do this weekend. There's this new orangutan at Safari World, and I bet he's dying to make friends."

"I'd love to hear about your monkey pals, Screech, but I have to make a phone call," Zack said. "My mom might want me to stop at the grocery store on the way home. Be right back."

When Zack walked off, Screech suddenly hit the table, sending a nacho flying into Jessie's lap. "Hey, I just remembered something!" he exclaimed.

"Me, too," Jessie said, scraping guacamole off her jeans. "It's time to do my laundry."

"You guys, how could we have forgotten?" Screech continued. "The Palisades Historical Scavenger Hunt starts this weekend! Mr. Loomis told us about it in history class today."

Slater grinned. "I'll show you how we could forget." He dropped his head on his chest and began to snore loudly.

Jessie poked him. "Wake up, you caveman. Actually, Screech is right. It *does* sound like fun."

"Sure, if you like history," Lisa said. She dropped her head and began to snore, too.

Jessie laughed. "Where's your civic pride?" she asked.

"I think I left it in my other pants," Slater said.

"Come on, guys," Screech said. "It'll be a blast. We've got to do it."

In honor of the four hundred and fiftieth anniversary of the founding of the city of Palisades by the Spanish, a citywide historical scavenger hunt had been announced. The hunt was open to all high school students. They could enter in pairs, and Mr. Loomis had urged the class to give it a try.

"You get extra credit for joining," Screech reminded them.

"You sure could use some extra credit," Jessie said to Slater. "You might even venture into unknown territory, Slater—the world of the B average."

Slater shuddered. "Sounds scary. I think I'll stick with my Cs."

"And there's the five-hundred-dollar prize offered to the winners by the chamber of commerce," Jessie continued.

Slater sat up. "Five hundred dollars? How did I miss that?"

"It must have been during your nap," Jessie said.

"There's also an honorary membership with the Palisades Historical Society," Screech said.

"Who cares? I'm talking cold, hard cash," Slater said. He turned to Jessie. "What do you say, momma? Let's forget tennis and try it. After all, you need a man for a scavenger hunt. Boys are definitely better than girls at hunting—even when it comes to historical facts. It's in our genes. Men have been hunters since the beginning of time."

"Wait a second, Slater," Jessie said, annoyed. "A scavenger hunt involves *thinking* and *reasoning*. You know—those skills that have absolutely nothing to do with a bunch of Neanderthals running around with sticks."

"You can never admit when you might need a man, Jess," he said. "It just so happens that men also make the best diggers for information. All the great journalists are men."

Lisa and Jessie sat up indignantly. "That's because until recently, women used to be confined to the society pages," Jessie said angrily.

"Ever hear of Diane Sawyer, chump?" Lisa asked sweetly.

Slater crossed his muscular arms. "I still say that when you pit men against women in a contest of *any* kind, men will win. Right, Screech?"

Screech frowned. "Gee, I don't know. Belinda Towser won the science fair gold ribbon three years in a row. And last year, Jennifer Ralston won the Bayside Triathalon. Didn't she beat *you*, Slater?"

"I had a sore knee," Slater growled.

"Hmmm, contests. There's Miss America, of course—" Screech continued.

Slater nudged him with his elbow. "Whose side are you on?" he muttered. "Or should I say, which side of your face would you like your nose to be on?"

Screech crossed his scrawny arms. "I agree with you, Slater. Absolutely."

Jessie and Lisa exchanged glances. A thought seemed to spring from Jessie's brain to Lisa's. They both grinned at each other and nodded.

"Oh, really?" Jessie asked. "Well, prove it."

"Any day, momma," Slater said. "You name the time. You name the place. You name the game."

"The scavenger hunt. City hall, tomorrow morning, ten A.M. Girls against the boys," Jessie said crisply.

Slater hesitated. He hadn't meant it to go this far. He didn't know much about early California history. Jessie was a total brain. She'd won the history medal this year. He must be crazy. But he couldn't back down now.

"What's the matter, Slater?" Jessie taunted. "Cat got your tongue?"

"Not at all," Slater said. Suddenly, he wished his gorgeous girlfriend wasn't so smart. "I just don't want to embarrass you, Spano."

"That's really nice of you," Jessie cooed. "Does that mean you won't take the challenge? Or should I say, you're *afraid* to?"

"You're on, momma," Slater said. "Get ready to be pulverized."

"Girls against the boys," Lisa said with satisfaction.

Screech nodded. "And may the best man win!"

Chapter 2

▲ ▼ ▲ ▼ ▲

Zack was beaming when he turned from the phone. But when he got to the table, he heaved a heavy, world-weary sigh. "I'm back, peons," he said as he slid back into his seat. He looked around the Max. "What a dump! And those nachos, pleh!"

"What's up with you, Zack?" Jessie asked. "Who made you king all of a sudden? And, anyway, what's wrong with nachos? Five minutes ago, you loved them."

"Not anymore," Zack said. "I'm developing a taste for caviar."

"Little, slimy fish eggs?" Lisa asked with a shudder. "Count me out."

"And what about the momma fish, Zack?" Screech asked in a wobbly voice. "What happened when she came back to her nest and found her babies gone? Did you ever think about her, Zack, as those little baby eggs were sliding down your greedy throat?"

"Lighten up, Screech," Zack said. "I haven't tasted them *yet*. But it's only a matter of time."

"What are you talking about, preppy?" Slater asked. "Caviar isn't in your budget."

Zack leaned over the table. "So what? I can charge it on my very own account at the Half Moon Country Club."

"You *wish*," Lisa said. "That's the most exclusive club in Palisades."

"Exactly why my father joined it today," Zack replied. He put his hand over his heart. "Dear old dad."

The rest of the gang exchanged glances. "Are you saying that your father joined the Half Moon Country Club?" Jessie asked incredulously.

"Bingo!" Zack said. "You get the car *and* the frost-free refrigerator! Remember that big backer Dad's been trying to get for his business? Well, he's on the board at the club. Dad figured a few rounds of golf with the man wouldn't hurt. So that means the Morris clan is now fully instated at Half Moon."

"Oh, my gosh," Lisa said. "I definitely have to overhaul my wardrobe. You *are* going to invite me as a guest, aren't you?"

Zack waved a hand. "Sure. But first I want to take Kelly. I can see us now, lazing by the pool. Snapping our fingers for another iced tea. Then strolling over for a set of tennis on one of the many courts. And I'm sure Kelly will fit right in with the ritzy country club crowd."

Jessie exchanged a glance with Lisa. They had no doubt that Kelly would fit in just about anywhere. She was a sweet, down-to-earth girl. But her family didn't have much money. How would the richest kids in Palisades react to that? And Kelly liked everyone she met, practically. She made excuses for bullies and said that gossips were just insecure. But the one kind of person she couldn't take was a snob. How would *she* react to the ritzy kids at the club?

"Right, Zack," Lisa said. "I'm sure Kelly will fit right in."

"I can't wait," Zack said dreamily. "And I can't wait to tell Kelly."

"Looks like you don't have to," Slater observed. "Here she comes."

Kelly burst through the door of the Max and ran toward them, her silky dark hair flying.

"I have the most fantastic news!" she told them, her blue eyes sparkling. "I got a job!"

She slid into the seat next to Zack. "I couldn't believe it. Even though I don't have any waitressing experience, the manager really liked me."

"Where's the restaurant, Kelly?" Lisa asked.

"Can we get free food?" Slater wondered.

Kelly giggled. "I don't think so. It's a real

snooty place. I'll have to wait on a bunch of snobby fat cats, but I bet I'll rake in the tips. It's the dining room at the Half Moon Country Club!"

Everyone except Zack and Kelly started to laugh. Slater stood up and made a mock bow in front of Kelly.

"Madam, may I introduce you to your first customer?" he asked, a wicked gleam in his brown eyes. "This is snobby fat cat Zack Morris!"

"Wait a second," Kelly said, looking around at their faces. "Do you mean—"

Zack clapped a hand to his forehead. "Whatever will Mummy say? I'm dating the help!"

▲   ▼   ▲

On Saturday morning, Kelly was so nervous that she woke up early and got to the restaurant a half hour before her shift started. Her parents had gone away on a trip, taking her younger brothers and sisters with them, and she'd been nervous about oversleeping without her mother there to make sure she didn't. She couldn't depend on her older brothers. They'd either forget about her, or else they'd come by and pound on her door and give her a heart attack.

Her new manager, Bradford Porterhouse, was already there. He smiled when he saw her.

"Showing up early to impress the boss?" he asked, his green eyes twinkling.

Bradford was definitely not like Gus Vance at

the Yogurt 4-U, Kelly reflected. Gus's belly hung over his stained apron, and his idea of a big hello was a grunt. Bradford was about twenty-five and handsome. He was definitely no Mr. Vance.

"Not really," Kelly answered, shrugging out of her linen blazer. "I was nervous about being late."

"Well, this will give you time to see if the uniform fits," Bradford said. "Here." He handed her a folded uniform and a key. "This key is to the women's locker room. To get there, go through the kitchen, a few steps down the hall, first door on your right. You can take any locker that's open and leave your clothes and purse there. The locker room is just for women, so you'll have privacy." He leaned closer and winked. "I'm the only other person with a key."

Kelly smiled and headed off. That had been a weird thing to say, but she guessed Bradford had a more sophisticated kind of humor.

In the locker room, Kelly quickly changed into her black uniform. It was a little baggy, but she tied the starched white apron tightly around her waist, and that helped a little. She went back to the dining room and found Bradford in the service area for the waitresses, writing on a clipboard.

"Whoa," he said when he saw her. "You sure do nice things for that uniform, Kelly."

Kelly blushed. "Uh, thank you. It's a little big."

He looked her up and down very slowly. "Yeah, it could be a little tighter in some places."

Kelly didn't know what to say, so she just smiled again. She guessed that Bradford liked to tease people. His tone was really friendly, though. If Mr. Vance had said that to her at the Yogurt 4-U, she would have socked him with a banana. Besides, it was her very first day. She really wanted to impress Bradford.

Suddenly, Bradford was all business. "Okay, this is your time card," he said. "I've already filled in your name. You need to write down the time you come in and the time you leave. Then stick it in this slot, here. Your first duty will be to make sure the busboys have set up your station correctly. Then make the iced tea and coffee. Maria Elena can show you if you don't know how. She's our senior waitress."

"Okay, Mr. Porterhouse," Kelly said, nodding. "I think I've got it so far."

"Please, Kelly," he said, smiling. "Mr. Porterhouse is my dad. Call me Brad, okay?"

Kelly smiled. "Okay. Brad."

He put his hand on her shoulder and patted it. "I'm sure you'll do just fine. Don't be nervous."

"I'll try not to be," Kelly said.

"Ah, here's your partner in crime. Buenos días, Maria Elena," Brad called.

A petite, dark-haired girl walked up, dressed

in a waitress uniform. Brad introduced her to Kelly.
"I have some paperwork to do in my office," he
said. "Kelly, if you have any problems—and I mean
any little thing—you come and see me. Okay?"

"Okay, Mr.—I mean, Brad," Kelly said.

Brad walked off. "Brad seems nice," Kelly
said. "Is he a good boss?"

"He's only been here a few weeks," Maria
Elena said, pouring water into the coffee machine.
"His father is a big deal here at the club, and he got
him the job. I heard that Brad has had trouble
starting a career. He seems okay so far." Maria
Elena's dark eyes danced. "It's the customers you
have to watch out for," she said in a conspiratorial
whisper.

Kelly giggled. "As long as they tip well, I'll put
up with anything."

Maria Elena rolled her eyes. "You won't say
that if you get the Triple A's."

Kelly frowned. "The Automobile Association
of America?"

Maria Elena laughed. "No. Amber, April, and
Andrea. Three girls who are used to getting things
their way. Remember, the customer is always right.
And that goes triple for the Triple A's. Actually,
Amber is Brad's sister. Maybe we should give *him*
her table. All I know is that you can't do anything
right for those three. And then they're the worst
tippers in the world!"

"They sound awful," Kelly said worriedly. "I'll probably spill iced tea all over them."

"I hope so," Maria Elena said, and they laughed. "Don't worry. You probably won't get them. Their favorite table is in my station. You get the Dead Zone, since you're new."

"The Dead Zone?" Kelly asked. "That sounds kind of scary."

Maria Elena laughed. "All the waitresses call the front tables the Dead Zone. They're the tables that get filled last. So if the restaurant isn't crowded, you might have a couple of free tables. Nobody wants to sit at the tables in front. They want to sit overlooking the golf course. Actually, it's probably better for you. It will give you a chance to get the hang of things."

Kelly frowned. "But will I always be stuck in the Dead Zone? I won't make much in tips."

"That's a problem," Maria Elena said. "I'm trying to get Brad to rotate the waitress stations. It's only fair. Listen, if the Triple A's come in today and you happen to get them, just let me know. I'll take their table. You shouldn't have to deal with them on your first day. Now, we'd better get started," she said. "I don't want to test Brad's good nature."

For the next hour, Maria Elena showed Kelly the ropes. She showed her how to use the coffee machine and the iced tea maker, and to keep an eye on the milk pitchers on her tables. She introduced

Kelly to Nolan, the cook, warning the big man teasingly to be nice to Kelly or he'd have to answer to her. Maria Elena was generous and kind and very efficient. She had been a waitress for four years, since she was fifteen, and it showed.

Customers started to drift into the restaurant. Some were coming back from a game of golf and were starved for eggs and bacon. Some looked like they had just rolled out of bed and asked for coffee *immediately*. Soon Kelly was on the run. Maria Elena helped her when she could. She filled her water glasses for her and remembered table seven's catsup when Kelly forgot it three times.

"Don't worry," Maria Elena told her. "You're doing just fine. Really."

Kelly had never been so busy in her life. She was constantly moving, taking orders, totaling checks, filling her milk pitchers and sugar bowls, hearing Nolan ring the bell three times, which meant she had to dash to the kitchen pass-through before her orders got cold. She filled pastry baskets and coffee cups. She wiped off tables and babies' chins.

"If you think this is bad, just wait until lunch," Maria Elena said, flashing a grin as she raced off to refill the iced tea pitcher.

Every table except one was taken in Kelly's section and table five had sent back his eggs twice when three blond-haired girls entered the dining room. Kelly overheard them as she looked for the strawberry jam in the service area. Marmalade *just wouldn't do* for table four.

"Bummer," one of the girls said. "Our regular table is taken."

"And look who has it, Andrea. Dink Dunkerson," another one said. "How gross. That man must have at least three and a half chins."

"I guess it has to be this table in the front, Amber," the first one said. "At least it's by a window."

"Let's go, April," the last girl said. "I'll *die* if I don't get my Perrier."

The names seemed to toll inside Kelly's brain like warning bells. *Amber. April. Andrea.* She looked around for Maria Elena, but she was busy taking an order from a table of ten. The terrible Triple A's were heading straight for Kelly's station. She was on her own!

Chapter 3

▲ ▼ ▲ ▼ ▲

"Isn't this exciting?" Jessie asked Lisa. They were standing in City Hall Park, surrounded by other students waiting for the scavenger hunt to begin. Jessie's hazel eyes shone as she scanned the park. "Just look at all this civic pride!"

Lisa yawned. Behind her big sunglasses, her eyes were closed. "Wow," she said dully.

Jessie poked her. "Wake up, partner. Your brain needs to function this morning."

"But it's Saturday," Lisa complained. "And it's so *early*."

"It's ten o'clock!" Jessie protested, laughing.

"My point exactly," Lisa said. "On Saturdays, these dainty feet do not hit the floor until eleven-fifteen. And then they go straight to a hot shower for twenty minutes."

"Well, you'd better wake up," Jessie advised.

"The honor of the entire female sex is at stake, remember?"

"Right," Lisa said, yawning again. "Do you think they'll hand out breakfast with the clues? I'm kind of hungry."

"Shhh," Jessie said. "There go Slater and Screech. Darn. I was hoping they'd be late."

"Are you kidding?" Lisa asked. "Screech wouldn't miss a second of this. He's taping it for his extra-credit project for Mr. Loomis."

Just then, Damon Frederick, the president of the Palisades Historical Society, came out of the city hall and stood on the steps in front of a microphone. "Welcome, boys and girls," he said. "I have in my hand the first set of clues in the Palisades Historical Scavenger Hunt. Remember, we are commemorating the four hundred and fiftieth anniversary of the founding of Palisades. All of the clues will have to do with the glorious history of our great town. You will receive the first set of clues today. You must return here at five o'clock sharp to submit your answers. Then, next Saturday, we'll meet here at the same time for the next, and final, set of clues. The winners will be announced at the Half Moon Ball at the country club Saturday night. Whichever team gets the most correct answers wins the grand prize of memberships to the Palisades Historical Society and five hundred dollars!"

Everyone cheered. "The envelopes are now

being handed out," Mr. Frederick announced. "Do *not* open them until I give the signal. Anyone caught opening an envelope before the signal will be disqualified."

Jessie flung a look at Slater. She wouldn't put it past him to sneak a peek at the clues. He looked over the heads at her, too. He didn't trust her! Jessie tossed her long curls and grabbed an envelope. She tapped it impatiently against her leg.

"All right," Mr. Frederick said. "You may begin! Good luck, everyone."

Jessie eagerly tore open the envelope. Lisa slipped off her sunglasses and peered over her shoulder. "What does it say?"

Jessie read it out loud. Around her, other kids were doing the same. "MISSION IMPOSSIBLE: FIND THE CELLULAR PHONE BACK IN 1772."

"Cellular phone? In seventeen seventy-two?" Lisa asked. "I don't get it. What does it mean?"

"I don't know," Jessie said, frowning. "I don't have the slightest idea, Lisa!"

"Now, don't panic," Lisa said, gazing around her. "Nobody else does, either."

It was true. Everyone else looked as puzzled as they did. Jessie looked over at Slater. His curly haired head was still bent over the paper.

"Look at him," she said to Lisa in a low voice. "That bonehead will never figure it out."

But Jessie was horrified when, suddenly,

Slater smacked the paper and whispered something to Screech. Screech nodded, and the two of them ran across the grass to where Slater's car was parked. They jumped in and roared off.

"Well, will you look at that," Lisa said slowly. "The bonehead is ahead!"

▲   ▼   ▲

Slater chortled as he drove off. "Did you see Jessie's face?" he asked Screech. "She looked green!"

"Do you think she's coming down with something?" Screech asked, twisting around. "Maybe we should go back."

"No way," Slater said, speeding up. "I'm leaving her in the dust."

"Um, that brings me to a question, Slater," Screech said. "Where are we going, exactly?"

"I have no idea," Slater admitted.

"You mean you haven't figured out the clue?" Screech squeaked.

"Are you nuts?" Slater asked, turning the corner and parking the car. "That clue is *hard*. A cellular phone in Seventeen seventy-six? That doesn't make any sense. They didn't even have regular telephones back then."

"Seventeen seventy-two," Screech corrected.

"Excuse me," Slater said. "Not that it makes any difference. They didn't have telephones in Seventeen seventy-two, either. And what do they mean by 'mission impossible'? I *know* they didn't have television, either."

"So we're just as stuck as Jessie and Lisa," Screech said with a sigh.

Slater shook his curls. He grinned. "Wrong, partner. When it comes to the game of intimidation, we're way ahead."

▲   ▼   ▲

Amber Porterhouse tapped her glass. "I asked for *lemon* with my Perrier. Not lime. And you put ice in my glass!"

"I'll get you another," Kelly said cheerfully. "But we're out of lemons. We had a run on iced tea this morning," she explained.

Amber sighed. "Well, that's not my problem, is it?"

Andrea giggled. "It's probably Brad's. He's in charge of ordering supplies, right?"

"Can I get you girls anything else?" Kelly asked.

April pushed her sandwich across the table. "You might try a decent sandwich. This egg salad tastes funny."

"It was just made fresh this morning," Kelly said, holding onto her bright smile.

"I don't care," April said. "I don't feel like egg salad, anyway. Just bring me a salad with house dressing."

"Fine," Kelly said, taking the plate.

"And don't charge me for that!" April said.

Kelly looked down at the sandwich. April had eaten more than half of it. She knew the girl was testing her. But what could she do? *The customer is always right,* Maria Elena had told her. *And that goes triple for the Triple A's.*

"I wouldn't dream of it," Kelly said. "I just hope the half you *did* eat doesn't make you sick."

"Hey," April said, confused. "What—"

"I'll be right back with your salad." Kelly hurried off. *What a bunch of whiny snobs!* she thought furiously as she dumped the half sandwich into the trash. *They're as bad as the girls at Miss Fopp's School for Young Ladies.* But, unfortunately, they weren't *that* much worse than her other customers. Some of them had been nice. But, mostly, these people didn't think it was necessary to smile or say thank you. They just kept chewing.

Kelly giggled. It reminded her of the summer she was twelve, when she'd helped her uncle Dan on his farm. She didn't get any thanks from the cows, either.

She brought back a house salad for April and a new Perrier for Amber, then had to run and get lemonade for Andrea. But Andrea thought the lemonade was too tart, so Kelly went back for an iced tea. Then Andrea said her hamburger was too rare. April said she'd asked for dressing on the side, even though she hadn't. Kelly ran back for another salad.

By the time the Triple A's had finished their lunch, Kelly felt as though she'd been through three aerobics classes in a row. But at least they had run up a big bill! Kelly hurried to the table when they'd gone. They'd signed the bill on Amber's account, but Amber had forgotten to write in a tip.

"Having fun yet?" Maria Elena whispered as she came up with a loaded tray.

"I'm ready to drop," Kelly murmured. "But at least my shift is almost over. It's got to be two o'clock by now."

"What are you talking about, Kelly?" Maria Elena said. "It's only noon."

▲   ▼   ▲

"Hmmmm. 'Cellular phone.' Maybe the phone company is in a historic building," Lisa suggested. She and Jessie were sitting cross-legged on the grass, tossing ideas back and forth.

"It's not," Jessie said, shading her eyes from the sun. "I had to go down to pay our phone bill once when my mom forgot. It's brand-new. Maybe we need to check what was around here in Seventeen seventy-two."

"I can't imagine," Lisa said gloomily. "There aren't any buildings in Palisades that are that old. The town hadn't even been founded then. The land probably belonged to the Spanish, right? There were just pueblos and a few missions. I don't remember, really. I kind of zoned out when Mr. Loo-

mis gave that lecture. It was on the same day that
I had a date with Billy Thorndike." Lisa stretched
out her legs. "That's why this extra-credit deal
probably isn't a bad idea. I daydream a lot in Loomis's class. And speaking of dreaming . . ." She
turned her face to the sun and closed her eyes.

Suddenly, Jessie's face cleared. "Lisa, you're a
genius."

Lisa opened one eye. "I am?"

" 'Mission'!" Jessie said. She looked around,
then lowered her voice. "What's the oldest building
for miles around?"

Lisa sat up slowly. "The Santa Teresa Mission," she said. "Of course! But what about the
cellular phone?"

Jessie jumped to her feet. "I don't know. But
I bet the answer is at the mission. Come on."

The mission was only about fifteen minutes
east of town. Jessie pulled into a parking space and
scanned the lot, looking for Slater's '57 Chevy.
"They're not here," she said happily. "We lucked
out! They're probably totally confused."

"Or else *we* are," Lisa pointed out.

Jessie and Lisa hurried into the mission, which
had been built in 1772. They toured it quickly, peering at crude tools used for tending the garden and
sketches of what the Indians and the priests had
worn. There was a small restored chapel and the
replica of the original kitchen. But there was nothing

that seemed to have anything to do with the clue.

"Let's check out the monks' bedrooms," Jessie said. "I think Mr. Loomis told us that they're called cells."

"Cells," Lisa breathed. "Maybe that has something to do with the cellular phone!"

"That's right!" Jessie said.

The two girls hurried toward the cell of Father Guadalupe Arguella, the founder of the mission.

Lisa examined the replica of his hooded robe, which was hanging on a hook near the door. "This is it!" she cried.

"What?" Jessie breathed.

"This is *exactly* the kind of beach cover-up I'm looking for!" Lisa said. "I think I'd like it in terry cloth, though. And this color is kind of drab."

"Lisa, can you *please* stop thinking about clothes for thirty seconds?" Jessie pleaded. She began to prowl through the small room, examining the various displays. Suddenly, she swiveled and stared at Lisa. "I found it!" she hissed. "Here!"

"Where?" Lisa asked. She went closer and examined a small copper bell mounted on the wall. "This?"

"Read the card next to it," Jessie instructed. " 'This bell was attached to a long wire that ran out into the kitchen garden. Father Arguella was an avid gardener. This was how the other priests summoned him to prayer.' "

"A *cell*ular phone," Lisa said with a laugh. "This *is* it." She frowned. "But what do we do now? We can't rip the bell off the wall."

"I bet there's a replica of it in the gift shop," Jessie said. "Come on."

They hurried to the gift shop. Sure enough, there was "Father Arguella's bell" for two ninety-five. Jessie and Lisa bought the bell and hurried out of the mission.

"We're ahead of them!" Jessie crowed as they headed for the car. "Slater will never figure out that clue."

"Wanna bet?" Lisa asked. She pointed with her chin. Slater and Screech were just getting out of Slater's car. When they saw Jessie and Lisa, they walked up to them.

"You girls look worried," Slater said. "Afraid you're falling behind already?"

"Dream on," Jessie shot back. "We're already on the second clue."

Slater looked crestfallen. "You are?"

"We are," Lisa said. "And I'd say good luck to you, but I really wouldn't mean it."

"So you're in the lead," Slater said with an easy shrug. "Big deal. Girls always give up. Men have endurance."

"I even *wear* Endurance Cologne," Screech said.

"Keep talking, you guys," Jessie said. "We're

number one!" She raised her arm to point a finger at Slater, but she forgot she was holding the bag. Inside, the bell gave a faint tinkle.

"What was that?" Slater asked suspiciously.

"Nothing," Jessie said quickly.

"It was a bell!" Slater exclaimed. "That's the answer to the cellular phone clue. Come on, Screech." He leaned over and gave Jessie a big, smacking kiss on the cheek. "Thanks for the hint, momma. Now I know you still care."

"I don't!" Jessie yelled after him. But Slater and Screech were already inside the mission.

Jessie stamped her foot in frustration. "I gave them the first clue on a silver platter!" she cried to Lisa.

"You bought a silver platter, too?" Lisa said. "Is it nice? Maybe I should check out that gift shop again."

Chapter 4

▲ ▼ ▲ ▼ ▲

Kelly sank down on a stool in the country club kitchen. All of the cooks were out on their breaks. They'd be back in an hour to start prepping for dinner. Maria Elena had hurried off to her class at the local community college. It felt good to be alone.

She eased off one white shoe, then rubbed her foot. She groaned.

Brad appeared in the kitchen doorway. "Tough first day?"

Kelly managed a smile. "It wasn't too bad."

"Liar," Brad teased.

Kelly laughed. "Okay. Let me put it this way: If this day was a boat, it would be the *Titanic*."

"Waitressing is one of the hardest jobs in the world," Brad said, sitting down next to her. "Becoming a restaurant manager has given me total respect for the profession."

"Me, too," Kelly said. "Maria Elena makes it look so easy."

"You did well," Brad said. "I was watching you, Kelly. You have a way with the customers."

"As long as I don't forget to bring them their catsup for the third time," Kelly said. Then she realized she was talking to her boss. Maybe she shouldn't have said that. But Brad was so friendly, for a moment she'd forgotten.

But he just laughed. "You'll get the hang of it, I promise." His green eyes glowed as he looked at her. "You're a natural."

Kelly wouldn't go *that* far. But it was a nice thing to say, anyway. "Thanks."

"Listen, Kelly. I was wondering . . . do you like Chinese food?"

"Love it," Kelly said. "Are we going to have Chinese night or something?"

Brad laughed. "No. Actually, I want you to *eat* it, not serve it. With me. Tonight."

"Gosh, Brad, I don't know," Kelly said. "I mean, it's really nice of you to ask. But I'm going steady with someone."

"Going steady? What a hoot," Brad said. "Come on, Kelly. That's kid stuff."

Kelly smiled. "Not to me. As a matter of fact, I'm supposed to meet him by the pool in a few minutes."

"Oh." Brad frowned. "Well, you'd better run along then, Kelly."

"I think I'd better," Kelly said, jumping up. "I'll see you tomorrow for Sunday brunch."

"Right," Brad said, looking away.

Kelly rushed off to the locker room to change. She hoped she hadn't offended Brad. But even if she *wasn't* going steady with Zack, she wouldn't have gone out with him. He was cute, but he was a little too old for her. But she didn't want to tell him that. It might hurt his feelings.

Kelly climbed into her red tank suit and shorts. She brushed out her hair, slipped her feet into sandals, and she was ready. Throwing her canvas tote over her arm, she hurried to the pool.

She saw Zack standing on the edge of the pool, and she waved, but he didn't see her. He dived in and surfaced. Then he swam over to a group of girls who were standing in the shallow end. She heard the sound of their laughter.

Grinning, Kelly walked toward them. *Leave it to Zack to make friends with all the girls,* she thought ruefully. She didn't mind, but she also wasn't sorry to have the opportunity to stake out her territory.

Zack looked up as she came to the edge of the pool. His face lit up as he swept his wet blond hair off his forehead. "Kelly! Finally! I thought you'd never make it."

"You don't *look* like you're suffering much," Kelly teased.

"Oh, but I am," Zack said. "I think I'm getting

a sunburn. But I *did* manage to meet some dynamite people. Kelly, meet my new friends. New friends, meet my girlfriend."

"Girlfriend?" one of the girls said. Kelly finally turned her attention to them. Her heart sank when she saw who they were.

"This is Amber, April, and Andrea," Zack said. "They call themselves the Triple A's. Isn't that wild?"

"Hey, weren't you our *waitress*?" Andrea asked.

Kelly nodded. "I work in the dining room."

"Oh," April said. Her eyes flicked up and down Kelly.

"Sorry about the lemon," Kelly told Amber with a grin. She'd at least *try* to be friendly, she decided.

Amber tossed her blond hair. "Hey, don't mention it. I coped."

April giggled. "I can't believe you're dating our waitress, Zack."

"It was Kelly's first day," Zack said fondly. "How did it go?"

"Okay," Kelly said. She'd love to tell him about her very worst customers, but somehow, she didn't think it was the right time.

Amber shot Kelly a dismissing glance. "Come on, Zack," she said. "You promised to show me that dive."

"Right," Zack said. "Come on, Kelly. Jump in. The water's great."

Slowly, Kelly walked over to leave her gear on Zack's chaise longue. She slipped out of her shorts as she heard April's squeal and Andrea's high-pitched laugh. Those girls had looked right through her as if she didn't exist. And if Kelly's instincts were right, Amber was definitely interested in Zack as more than a friend.

Guys were so dumb sometimes, Kelly thought as she waded into the cool water. How could Zack actually *like* these girls? Why couldn't he see through them? They just froze her out right in front of him. She felt like a Popsicle.

As she struck off across the pool, Kelly had to suppress a sigh. Zack hadn't been exactly delighted when she'd told him she was going to look for a second job. He'd thought it would really cut into the time they spent together. But when she'd gotten this job, he'd thought waitressing at the club was the perfect solution. This way, he'd said, the job wouldn't come between them. They'd have plenty of chances to see each other.

Kelly frowned as she swam up and Andrea and April turned their backs to her, separating her from Zack and Amber. She treaded water, thinking. *My job won't come between Zack and me,* Kelly realized. *But maybe the country club will.*

▲   ▼   ▲

"Let me see the clue, Screech," Slater said in the parking lot of the Santa Teresa Mission. "You've been staring at the paper for ten minutes, and you haven't figured anything out."

"Yes, I have," Screech said. "I figured out that they used a laser printer, not a dot matrix."

Slater snatched the paper from Screech's grasp. He frowned as he read the clue again.

EVEN PACKED LIKE SARDINES, SHOPPING CAN BE FUN! BRING BACK A BAG TO PROVE IT.

"I know one thing," Slater said. "If the clue has to do with shopping, Lisa is going to figure it out faster than I can scarf down a cheeseburger."

"She hasn't done it yet," Screech said, peering over the cars toward Jessie's blue Toyota. "They're still sitting there."

"Good," Slater said. "Now *think*, Screech!"

"I *am* thinking," Screech said. "But the only thing I can come up with is the shopping center a few miles from here that's in an old factory. The factory used to can fish, and it was renovated back in the seventies and turned into shops." Screech shrugged.

"What do you mean, that's *all* you can think of?" Slater exclaimed. "That's it! You figured out the clue. All we have to do is bring back a shopping bag or something." His fingers drummed on the steering wheel.

"So let's go," Screech said.

"In a second," Slater said. "If we figured it out so fast—"

"We?" Screech said pointedly.

"—you," Slater said grudgingly. "I just know that Lisa or Jessie will come up with it in a minute. I can't let that happen. This is our chance to get a big lead on them."

"But how?" Screech asked. "I guess I could jump up and down on Jessie's car hood to distract them. But Lisa hates my monkey impression. She thinks it's really immature."

"That's it!" Slater said.

Screech shook his head. "I won't do it, Slater. Not even for you. I can't jeopardize my relationship with Lisa."

"Screech, you don't *have* a relationship with Lisa," Slater pointed out.

"Not yet," Screech responded. "But I'm sure any year now, she'll realize that dating handsome hunks is pointless when she can have me."

"Right, Screech," Slater said. "But I wasn't asking you to do your monkey impression, anyway. *Distraction* is what I'm talking about. Here's what we're going to do. You sneak out of the parking lot and jump on the number six bus. It goes to the shopping center. You find a shopping bag with the canning factory's name printed on it. Meanwhile, I'll lead Jessie in the wrong direction. If I know my sneaky, competitive girlfriend, she'll take off after me and try to find the answer to the clue." Slater chuckled. "What a cheater!"

"*She's* a cheater?" Screech said. "But you're the one who—"

"That's enough, pencil neck," Slater growled. "I don't have a choice. I owe it to men everywhere to put that curly headed, arrogant smart aleck in her place."

▲   ▼   ▲

"Oh, no!" Lisa exclaimed. "It's happening again! Slater's taking off!"

"He can't!" Jessie cried. "Quick, Lisa, figure out the clue!"

"I can't!" Lisa wailed. "You know I hate sardines!"

Jessie's lips tightened. She could just glimpse the hood of Slater's Chevy heading out of the parking lot. "I can't let him win," she muttered. "I can't."

She turned on the engine and revved it.

"What are you doing?" Lisa asked. "Where are you going?"

"After him," Jessie said grimly as she wheeled toward the parking lot exit. "Did you see which way he turned?"

"Left," Lisa said. "But—"

"No buts," Jessie said. "I owe it to women everywhere to put that curly headed, arrogant smart aleck in his place. Don't lose him!"

"Jessie, this is cheating," Lisa said.

"No, it's not," Jessie said. "It's . . ."

"What?"

"Necessary," Jessie finished. "Now look!"

Lisa craned her neck. Slater was a few cars ahead. "He's heading west," she said.

Jessie nodded. "The clue must have something to do with the beach. Or fishing. Maybe he knows where there's sardine fishing. The clue is obviously biased toward men, Lisa. That's why we owe it to all the women in the scavenger hunt to do this."

"Right, Jessie," Lisa said dryly. She knew that even though Jessie was all for female solidarity, basically, she just wanted to cream Slater bad.

Slater passed through the edge of town and turned right on Ocean Boulevard. He headed toward Palisades Beach. Jessie followed his car for ten miles.

"Where can he be going?" Jessie wondered. "The fishing piers are south of here."

"I don't know," Lisa said. "But slow down. It's Saturday afternoon. We're going to run into beach traffic right after the Palisades Avenue turnoff. You don't want him to spot you."

Jessie let a yellow car get in front of her. In another mile, the traffic was clogged, and they were stopped dead.

"What are they doing now?" Jessie asked Lisa.

Lisa pulled on a baseball cap for a disguise. Then she raised herself right out the window to get a good look ahead. She dropped back into her seat with a crash. "This is weird," she said. "Slater is alone. Screech isn't in the car."

"Are you sure?" Jessie asked.

Lisa nodded. "Positive. Do you think he had to feed his hamster or something?"

Jessie shrugged. "Who knows what those two are up to."

"Who knows," Lisa agreed.

After a moment, Jessie and Lisa turned to each other.

"We've been had," Jessie said.

"I think so," Lisa agreed. "Slater just led us on a wild-goose chase, didn't he?"

"That snake!" Jessie said. "That double-dealing reptile!"

"Jessie, calm down," Lisa said. "We *did* follow him. Jessie?"

It was too late. Jessie flung open the car door and got out in the stalled traffic. She stalked down the line of cars and reached Slater's Chevy. He was listening to the radio and pounding the steering wheel with the beat. Jessie reached in and wrapped her hands around his throat.

"You slime!" she yelled. "You double-crossed me!"

Slater began to laugh. "It worked, didn't it?

Jessie? Aaaaarrggg." Choking and laughing, Slater pulled away. "You deserved it, momma," he said, bursting into another peal of uproarious laughter.

Jessie leaned into the car. "Do you know what this means, Slater?"

"Our tennis date is off?" Slater tried.

Her hazel eyes shot green sparks at him. "This means war," she said.

Chapter 5

▲ ▼ ▲ ▼ ▲

On Sunday morning, Kelly must have caught every red light on the way to the country club. Luckily, she was already wearing her uniform. If she'd had to change, she would have been super late. She raced into the dining room after throwing her bag in a locker—only two minutes late.

Brad looked at his watch. "It's a little early for you to start taking liberties, isn't it, Kelly?"

"I'm sorry," Kelly said. "I caught every red light between—"

"I don't want excuses," Brad said. "Just punctuality. If you didn't stay out late with your boyfriend, you'd be on time."

"I didn't stay out late," Kelly said quietly. "As a matter of fact, I was home early."

Brad turned his back. "Why don't you help Maria Elena set up? You don't want her to have to do everything, do you?"

"Of course not," Kelly said. She went over to the service area. "Boy, Brad's in a bad mood today," she murmured to Maria Elena.

"Really? I didn't notice," Maria Elena said. "Here, you can fill the creamers while I make the coffee."

Kelly plunged into her duties, and she quickly forgot Brad's scolding. The first customers began arriving, and soon she and Maria Elena were even busier than they'd been the day before. Sunday brunch was a big tradition at the club.

But Kelly began to notice that the busboy wasn't cleaning her tables as fast as he should. Often she had to hurriedly dump dishes into the gray rubber tub herself, then race to the kitchen to toss the dishes in the dishwasher.

What's going on? Kelly wondered worriedly. Yesterday, Armand had been super efficient. Today he was slower than Zack on Volunteer Cleanup Day at Bayside.

She managed to get a word with Armand later that morning. "Armand, I'm having problems keeping up with my tables," she said, smiling to show she didn't blame him. "Do you think you could give me a hand?"

"I'll try, Kelly," Armand said. "But Mr. Porterhouse assigned me to Maria Elena's tables today. I guess he told Peter to do yours."

"Oh, I'm sorry," Kelly said. "I'll talk to Peter, then."

But when Kelly found Peter, he told her that he was assigned to the back room of the restaurant. Nobody had been assigned to bus her station. Kelly looked around for Brad, but he was nowhere to be found. She didn't have time to track him down to tell him about the mix-up. She asked the two bus-boys to give her a hand when they could, and then raced back to take an order.

For the rest of the morning, Kelly worked as fast as she could, but she couldn't keep up with the mounting pile of dirty dishes on her tables. Customers began to complain. Some of them left without giving her any tips at all.

By the time her break arrived, Kelly felt ready to burst into tears. She walked quickly through the kitchen and pushed open the back door. Heaving a deep sigh, she sank onto the steps and took a breath of the fresh air.

The screen door squeaked behind her, and Kelly turned. Brad ambled down the steps and sat down next to her.

"It's a madhouse in there," he said. His tone was just as friendly as it had been yesterday. There wasn't a trace of the impatience she'd heard this morning. "How are you holding up?"

"I'm fine," Kelly said. "But I wanted to talk to you about—"

"Wait, Kelly," Brad interrupted hesitantly. "I think I know what you're going to say. I was a little short with you this morning."

"That wasn't it," Kelly said. "I forgot about this morning. It's fine, really."

"No, it's not," Brad said. "I wanted to apologize." He sighed and looked down at his shoes. "Sometimes I get a little overwhelmed. I'm new at my job, too. It can be nerve-racking."

"Sure," Kelly said. "I can understand that. *Boy*, can I understand that."

"I'm really under pressure here," Brad said. "My dad is a big wheel at the club. This is my last chance to prove to him that I can be a success at something. But it's really hard when everyone around me thinks of me as Nathan Jay Porterhouse's black sheep son. Can you understand that?"

The expression in Brad's clear green eyes was sad and a little lost. Kelly felt a surge of sympathy. "Of course I can," she said. "It must be really tough sometimes to be an important man's son."

"That's exactly it, Kelly," Brad said. He put his hand on her knee. "You really understand."

"Of course I do, Brad," Kelly said. She tried to move her leg so that Brad would take his hand off her knee. But he seemed really upset.

"I'd like to talk about this more with you," Brad said. "Are you busy tonight?"

Kelly couldn't believe it. Was Brad asking her for a date again? Or maybe he just wanted to talk, as friends. She shifted uncomfortably, not sure how to respond.

"Whoa, I'm getting boyfriend signals again," Brad said. "Does this guy have you on a leash?"

"No," Kelly said. "But we don't date anyone else. I don't *want* to. I love him."

"I see." Brad stood up, then lingered on the stairs. "So I heard you had a problem with the busboys today."

The abrupt shift to work topics threw Kelly off balance. "Yes, I did. I wanted to—"

"That's too bad. You must have done quite a bit of running around," Brad said. "Sorry to hear it."

Kelly smiled. "Oh, well. It couldn't be helped, I guess."

"Are you sure about that, Kelly?" Brad said.

Kelly's eyes clouded. "What do you mean?"

He leaned closer. "Let me know if you change your mind about tonight." Then he straightened up and turned around.

Brad went back up the stairs, whistling. The screen door slapped shut behind him. Kelly sat with his words still ringing in her ears.

Brad couldn't have meant what she thought he meant. *Are you sure about that, Kelly?* Had Brad deliberately made her job harder because she refused to go out with him?

No way, Kelly told herself firmly. *Nobody is that awful. Brad wouldn't do that.*

Would he?

▲   ▼   ▲

Yawning, Zack came downstairs on Sunday morning and walked into the sunny kitchen. His mother was at the stove, and he smelled sausage frying and coffee perking. "Wow," he said. "Sausage and waffles. My favorite Sunday breakfast."

Mrs. Morris grinned as she poured batter into the waffle iron. "What can I say? I got inspired."

Zack kissed his mother on the cheek and poured himself a glass of orange juice. " 'Morning, Dad," he said to his father, who was sitting at the kitchen table.

Mr. Morris smiled. For the first time in a long time, he looked happy and relaxed. "Good morning. How was your day at the club yesterday?"

"Great," Zack said, sitting opposite him. "I could definitely get used to this. I had a great swim, and I met some kids at the pool. How was your golf date with Mr. Mondo Honcho?"

"My golf game stunk up the joint," Mr. Morris admitted with a grin. "But we had a good meeting afterward. We're close, Son. We're very close. I think we might close the deal by next Saturday."

"That's fantastic news," Zack said. "When do I order my Porsche?"

"Dream on, hotshot," his mother said.

"Are you going to the club today?" Mr. Morris asked.

"Probably," Zack said. "I haven't thought about it yet. Kelly's working a double shift today. Then she's coming over and we're going to order a pizza."

Mr. Morris frowned. "I was hoping you'd eat dinner at the club with your mother and me tonight."

His mother put a plate of waffles and sausage down in front of Zack. "We're eating with Mr. and Mrs. Mondo Honcho," she murmured teasingly to Zack.

"Gosh, Dad, I wish you'd mentioned it earlier," Zack said. "I already made a date with Kelly."

"Couldn't you break it?" Mr. Morris asked. "It's only pizza. And I'll buy you steak at the club."

"Well—" Zack said. He didn't want to disappoint his dad, especially since they were getting along so well.

"That's enough, Derrick," Mrs. Morris said. "You don't want Zack to cancel *his* plans for *your* business dinner, do you?" She gave him a meaningful look.

Mr. Morris looked uncertain. Obviously, he *did* want Zack to cancel his plans. But Zack saw the steely look in his mother's blue eyes. You just didn't argue with Mom when she gave you that look. Even Zack's dad didn't.

"Of course not," Mr. Morris said. "Now, can I have another one of your delicious waffles, sweetheart?"

▲ ▼ ▲

"I'm glad you decided to keep our date, Jessie," Slater said as he and Jessie walked to the public tennis courts. "I was afraid you'd still be mad about yesterday."

"Why would you think that, Slater?" Jessie asked, swinging her racket.

"Gee, I don't know. Maybe it's because you hung up on me three times last night."

"Well, I'm over it," Jessie said. "I gave the whole situation a lot of thought. I think it's important that we don't let the bet interfere with our relationship."

Slater opened the gate to the court and let Jessie go in first. "Right on, momma," he said. "Just because we're competing in the scavenger hunt doesn't mean we still can't have a good time together."

"Exactly," Jessie said. She bounced the ball. "So let's have a nice, friendly game. Okay, sweetie?"

"You bet, pumpkin," Slater said. "Just a nice, friendly game."

Slater jogged over to the other side of the courts. Jessie served the ball, and he returned it in an easy lob.

"Good return," Jessie called.

"Thanks, Jess. It was an excellent serve."

"Thanks, sweetie pie."

They volleyed back and forth a few times. Then Slater smashed a return that zoomed past Jessie's racket.

"Good shot," she said, gritting her teeth. "A little sneaky since you know my backhand is weak. But it was a good shot."

"Just playing the game," Slater said.

Jessie slammed her next serve over the net. Slater ran for it and missed. "Good serve," he called in a strangled voice. "I *did* think we were playing a friendly game, but it was a good serve."

He tossed the ball back over the net a little harder than he meant to. It flew over Jessie's head, and she had to run to fetch it.

Jessie smiled as she walked back to serve. She smashed the ball right to Slater's weak side. "It *is* friendly, sweetie," she said. "I'm smiling. See?"

"Me, too," Slater said, baring his teeth.

"That's thirty love," Jessie called, naming the score.

"Love, my foot," Slater snarled under his breath. On his next return, he swung his racket back and whacked the ball to the edge of the baseline. As Jessie ran, she tripped over her racket and fell, skinning her knee.

"Sorry," Slater called. "Are you okay?"

"Fine," Jessie said. "Just fine." She picked up the ball and limped back to position.

Jessie served the ball. Slater smashed it back. They were locked in a deadly battle now. Jessie won the first game; Slater, the second. Jessie's arm began to ache. Slater began to gasp instead of breathe. But the score was tied, and neither one of them would give up.

"This game is the tiebreaker," Jessie called finally. "Prepare to die."

"I knew you couldn't do it!" Slater exclaimed. "I knew you couldn't have a friendly game."

"Don't be ridiculous," Jessie snarled. "You're the one who started to play rough. If you can't handle the heat, get off the court."

"Oh, *I* can handle it, all right," Slater shot back. "*You're* the one who's going to crack under the pressure. And I'm the one who's going to walk away with five hundred dollars next weekend. You just can't handle that, can you, Jessie? That's why you followed me all over Palisades yesterday. And that's why you're trying to beat me into the ground today."

"You're the one who tricked me!" Jessie exclaimed furiously.

"You're the one who fell for it," Slater said with a smirk. He looked around at the full courts next to them. "Hey, everyone! Meet my girlfriend, Jessie Spano, who has to be the best at everything.

She can't stand to lose, especially to me!"

Jessie's face flushed with anger as she wound up for her serve. She tossed the ball in the air, imagining it was Slater's little round head. She smashed the racket against it and heard the satisfying *thwack*.

Slater was still smirking as he turned to face forward again. But his mouth dropped open as he saw the bright green ball zoom in a straight, unwavering line across the net and hit him smack in the eye.

Chapter 6

▲ ▼ ▲ ▼ ▲

For the rest of the day, Kelly wondered if she had read something into Brad's comment that hadn't been there at all. He was as friendly as ever to her, and Armand was again busing her tables. It was as though their conversation hadn't taken place at all.

The dining room emptied out near the end of her shift. Kelly signed herself out on her time card and poured herself a glass of iced tea. With a sigh, she sat down at the bar. She was tired and glad the day was over. She couldn't wait to share a pizza with Zack tonight. If she saw another lobster-salad sandwich, she would hurl.

Brad came up behind her. "You know, you'd probably make better tips if you wore your skirt that way."

Kelly looked down and saw that her skirt had ridden up a little on her legs. It usually hit the top of her knees, but now it was miniskirt length. Even though she wore her own skirts that length, she felt embarrassed and quickly pulled it down.

Brad leaned against the wall. "Really, Kelly. If you shortened your hem, I bet you'd be a millionaire in no time."

Kelly smiled briefly and sipped her tea. She didn't know how to react to Brad's compliments. They made her uncomfortable, but she didn't want to hurt his feelings, either.

"Listen, come on back to my office, will you, Kelly?" Brad asked. "I want to talk to you about something."

Kelly hopped off the stool. "Sure."

She followed Brad to his tiny office in the rear of the restaurant. He closed the door behind her. Suddenly, Kelly felt a little uncomfortable. The office was so small. And Brad was standing too close. She backed up and hit the desk.

"The dinner shift next Saturday is going to be extra busy," Brad said crisply. "The Half Moon Ball is that night, and people will be eating here first. We close early, but it's going to be intense. I want you to be prepared. I'm going to put on an extra waitress and two extra busboys."

"Great," Kelly said, nodding. She was relieved that Brad actually wanted to talk business. But why did he have to tell her about Saturday night in his office?

"You're working Tuesday-night dinner, correct?" Brad asked. "How would you like to get out of the Dead Zone? I'd like to put you at Yvonne's station."

Yvonne was a pretty blond waitress who worked the back room. That was where the big wheels at the club had their regular tables.

"Wow," Kelly said. "Are you sure I'm ready? And are you sure that Yvonne won't mind?"

"I make the decisions, Kelly," Brad said. "And I think you're ready."

"Well, thanks," Kelly said. "I'll do my best."

There was a long pause. Kelly wondered if she should leave. Brad was just standing there, staring at her, smiling faintly.

"Brad? Is there anything else?"

"I hope your boyfriend tells you how pretty you are," Brad said.

"He does," Kelly said. "And he's probably waiting for me now, so, if there isn't anything else—"

Brad took a step closer. "I'm going to see *Improper Advances* tonight," he said, naming a popular film. "Would you like to come with me?"

Kelly had heard of the film. She knew it was rated NC-17. She felt herself blushing, and Brad's smile grew wider. He seemed to enjoy the fact that she was embarrassed.

"I can't," Kelly said. "I have—"

"—a date," Brad mimicked. "I know."

"Brad, can I go now?" Kelly asked. She wished he'd move away from the door.

"Sure," he said. But he didn't move.

"Can you move away from the door, please?" Kelly asked. She smiled nervously.

Brad moved over a few inches. He was still blocking the door, but she could reach the doorknob. Kelly hesitated.

Suddenly, there was a sharp rapping at the door.

"Who is it?" Brad asked in an annoyed tone.

"It's Maria Elena. I have a question for you."

Brad sighed and opened the door. Kelly quickly edged past him. "Good-night, you guys," she called. Maria Elena said good-night, but Brad said nothing.

Kelly ran to her locker. She grabbed her stuff and hurried to her car. That had been so weird. She had almost been scared of Brad. Was he aware that he made her feel that way? Or was he just awkward with girls? There had been something in his face tonight that seemed to tell Kelly he *enjoyed* making her feel uncomfortable.

Kelly pulled out of the country club gates. Biting her lip, she thought of her mother. If only she could talk to her! But she wouldn't be back until Sunday night. Kelly guessed she could talk to her older brothers. But it would be weird to confide in them. Kerry would make a joke, and Kirby might offer to beat Brad up. Kelly giggled. Maybe that wouldn't be so awful.

There was one other person she could confide in: Zack. He always knew how to make her feel better. And Zack always had a plan. Kelly felt cheered as she drove the remaining few blocks to his house. She couldn't wait to tell him what had been going on. He would help her figure it all out.

▲   ▼   ▲

Zack smiled when he opened the door and saw her in her uniform. "I'd like the roast beef, rare, and a baked potato," he said.

Kelly grinned. "I thought we were having pizza."

Zack leaned over and kissed her. "How was your day?"

"It was okay, I guess," Kelly said, walking into the comfortable Morris living room. "But this morning, my boss didn't assign a busboy to my tables. I was running all over the place."

"That's too bad," Zack said, sinking into the couch and pulling her down beside him.

"The thing is, I think there's a reason he didn't assign me a busboy," Kelly said.

"He's a lousy manager," Zack said. "He should have that stuff covered, I guess. Listen, Kelly, I had the most fantastic talk with my dad today." Zack and his father had remained at the kitchen table for about an hour after breakfast, sharing the Sunday paper and talking. They'd talked about normal stuff, sports and movies, whatever. Then they'd talked about his dad's dreams for his business. It was the most time Zack had spent with his dad in ages.

"That's great, Zack," Kelly said. She knew that Mr. Morris and Zack had trouble communicating. Zack was a little too unpredictable for his father sometimes. "Listen, it wasn't bad management—" she started.

"Kelly," Zack said, squeezing her hand, "Dad really confided in me today. It was so neat. He talked to me like another adult."

Kelly smiled softly at the look of quiet happiness in Zack's eyes. "I'm glad."

"He told me about how owning his own company was his dream. And he's so close to getting it. He's really glad that I've made friends at the club, especially with Amber."

Kelly frowned. "Why Amber?"

"Because she's the daughter of the big backer he's trying to get for his company," Zack explained. "I didn't even know it. Isn't that lucky?"

"Wait a second," Kelly said, sitting up. "Are you telling me that the backer your father is going after is—"

"Nathan Jay Porterhouse," Zack supplied.

"Mom and Dad are having dinner with the Porter-houses tonight."

"Zack, Nathan Jay Porterhouse is my boss's father!" Kelly exclaimed in horror. "Bradford Porterhouse."

"Your boss is Bradford Porterhouse?" Zack asked. "That's incredible."

"It is," Kelly said faintly. How could she tell Zack about her problems with Brad now?

"This is fantastic," Zack enthused. "I just know you'll make a great impression on him."

"I think I already have," Kelly said rue-fully.

Zack gave her a hug. "You're the best."

"That's not what I mean, Zack," Kelly said.

He pulled away and looked at her. "What *do* you mean, Kelly? Is something wrong? Did you get fired?"

She shook her head. "No. It's just that Brad seems kind of weird."

"Weird how?" Zack asked.

"Well, he compliments me a lot," Kelly said hesitantly. "He told me today that I'd make better tips if I'd shorten my skirt."

Zack laughed. "You probably would. That skirt is terminally ugly."

"He asked me out," Kelly said. "On a date."

Zack nodded slowly. "Well, I can understand that," he said. "I mean, you're a gorgeous girl,

Kelly. Any guy would want to date you. And Brad didn't know you were already dating the coolest guy around."

"I know, but he was angry when I said no," Kelly said.

"Are you sure you aren't overreacting, Kelly?" Zack asked. "Brad sounds like a normal guy to me. Maybe he shouldn't have asked you out, since you have a boyfriend. But you have to give the guy a break."

"I guess," Kelly said doubtfully.

"You can smooth over any situation," Zack told her. "Even a boss with attitude. Everybody likes you. Don't worry about it. I'm sure you can handle Brad. You'll end up wrapping him around your little finger, I just know it."

Kelly didn't say anything. Zack obviously didn't want to hear anything bad about Brad. It might mess up his father's plans. And she just couldn't tell Zack how uncomfortable Brad made her. She couldn't prove that he hadn't assigned a busboy to her tables just to punish her for refusing to date him. So he had stood a little too close to her in the office. And maybe he hadn't been quick enough to move away from the door. Zack would say it didn't mean anything. He'd say, *You're a pretty girl, Kelly. Brad just wanted to get close to you.* And maybe Zack would be right. And Brad *had* offered her the best station in the dining room, even though she'd turned him down for a date—twice.

Maybe she *was* overreacting, Kelly told herself as Zack went to phone for a pizza. Maybe the worst thing she could say about Brad was that he was a little too friendly. She'd just have to wait and see. And if she was right, she'd just have to handle it herself. She had seen Zack's face when he talked about his father. She couldn't spoil Mr. Morris's chances—and Zack's.

▲　　　▼　　　▲

Later that night, Zack was just turning off the TV in his room when he heard his parents come in downstairs. When he heard them in the upstairs hall, he poked his head out of his room.

"Have a good time, you guys?"

"Great," his mother said. She yawned. "I'm ready for bed, though."

"I'll be right in, honey," Mr. Morris told her. "I want to have a word with Zack." He followed Zack into his room.

"What's up, Dad?" Zack asked.

"Something happened at dinner I wanted to talk to you about," Mr. Morris said. "Do you know about the Half Moon Ball? It's at the club on Saturday night."

"Sure," Zack said. "All the kids at the club are talking about it."

"Well, apparently you made a big impression

on Amber," Mr. Morris said. "Mr. Porterhouse hinted to me that she'd love it if you'd ask her to the ball. Her boyfriend just broke up with her, and she's afraid no one will ask her. Nathan said he hates to see his little girl disappointed."

Zack sank down on the edge of his bed. "But, Dad, I was going to take Kelly. We're going steady. I can't ask another girl to the dance."

"Zack, I'd never ask you to do something that might hurt someone else," Mr. Morris said. "But if you explained things to Kelly, wouldn't she understand? You'd be going with Amber as a friend. It's just one dance, after all."

"That's true," Zack said.

"And Kelly is so understanding," Mr. Morris said. "I'm sure she'd realize how important this is for the family. But again, I wouldn't want you to jeopardize your relationship with Kelly. So if it's a problem, we'll just forget it."

Zack looked at his father. He'd done so many things to disappoint him. Zack's high school career wasn't exactly stellar. Half the time, he could barely keep a C average, and his father had been valedictorian at Bayside. Zack was kicked off the football team in ninth grade for dyeing all the uniforms purple. His father had been star quarterback.

All of Zack's life, his father had been fielding calls from his teachers listing the ways Zack Morris had messed up once again. Zack had had his share of lectures. But in the end, his dad was always in his corner. Now Zack had a chance to do something for him.

"All right, Dad," he said firmly. "I'll ask Amber to the ball. I'd be glad to. And I'm sure Kelly will understand."

Chapter 7

▲ ▼ ▲ ▼ ▲

On Monday morning, Lisa saw Jessie and Slater as she came up the walk to school. "Hey, fellow inmates," she greeted them. "Welcome back to the grind."

"You said it," Slater remarked. He looked glum behind his sunglasses. "I have an English quiz today. Tests should be outlawed on Mondays."

"And Fridays," Lisa agreed.

"I'll help you study, Slater," Jessie offered eagerly.

Lisa shot her a quick glance. She was glad to see that Jessie had forgiven Slater for what he'd done on Saturday. But she had to admit she was surprised. When it came to letting go of a grudge against Slater, Jessie was slower to move than Screech's pet tortoise, Boris. And Boris hadn't moved in *months*.

Slater frowned. "Don't worry about it, Jessie. I want to *pass* the quiz."

"So what did you do on Sunday afternoon, Jessie?" Lisa asked. "I called to see if you wanted to go shopping."

"I played tennis with Slater," Jessie said in a meek voice that wasn't like her.

"Now, that's what I like to see," Lisa said approvingly. "You guys aren't letting the scavenger hunt come between you. Sure, Slater pulled a dirty trick, but if we hadn't been trying to trick *him*, we wouldn't have fallen for it. I'd call it even. It's so silly to be competitive, isn't it?"

Slowly, Slater slid his sunglasses down his nose. Lisa gasped. Slater had a black eye!

"Tell that to *her*," he said to Lisa, indicating Jessie.

"Jessie, you punched out Slater?" Lisa asked Jessie in a horrified voice. She took another look at the shiner. "Wow. You must have some left hook."

"I didn't do it," Jessie said. "The tennis ball did. I mean, I hit the ball, but Slater's face got in the way."

"Hold the phone," Slater said. "My face got in the way? Maybe because you smashed the ball right at it."

"I told you I was sorry a million times," Jessie said. "I *am* sorry a million times. I didn't mean to smash your face like that."

"You'd better hope there're no scars, Spano," Slater said. "This face is valuable."

"You don't get scars from a black eye, Slater," Lisa said.

"Well, you never know," Slater said. He touched his eye gingerly. "You should have seen how hard Jessie hit that ball. Anybody got any aspirin?"

Suddenly, Jessie threw down her knapsack.

"I guess Jessie does," Lisa told Slater.

But Jessie only stamped her foot. "That's it!" she snapped. "I've had it! Ever since yesterday, all I've done is apologize to you. I bought you dinner last night. I baked you cinnamon rolls this morning. I drove you to school. I carried your books. I even offered to clean your tennis whites! I offered to do *laundry*, Slater! I've been bowing and scraping to you since it happened, and you keep rubbing it in! When are you going to forgive me?"

"When I don't look like I have a bull's-eye on my face!" Slater exclaimed. "You did this on purpose, Jessie!"

"I did not!" Jessie said. "I've told you that over and over again. But you know what I wish right now? I wish I had another shot!"

"Great!" Slater said. "That's just great! I *told* you she did it deliberately," he said to Lisa.

"You guys—" Lisa started.

"Only this time, I wouldn't use a tennis ball!" Jessie said. "I'd use my racket!" she picked up her knapsack and swung it over her shoulder, barely missing Slater's face.

"You see what I mean, Lisa?" he demanded. "She's trying to kill me!"

"Don't flatter yourself," Jessie said. "I wouldn't waste my time." She stalked off.

Angrily, Slater beat his fist against his leg. "Ow!" he yelled belligerently at Lisa.

"Slater, calm down and try thinking a minute," Lisa said. "Do you really think this stupid scavenger hunt is worth fighting with Jessie?"

"Talk to your friend. She's the one who started it," Slater said.

Lisa groaned. "You guys are unbelievable. You spend all your time arguing over who did what to who. Then you're surprised when you break up. You're like two speeding trains, heading toward each other on the same track. Neither one of you will switch off or even slow down. Then, when you have a wreck, all you can say is 'Duh, what happened?' "

"I don't need a lecture," Slater mumbled.

"It's not a lecture, it's a reality check," Lisa said crisply. "Look, it's this simple—what's more important to you? Winning a scavenger hunt or Jessie? Choose."

"It's not that simple," Slater argued.

"That's where you're wrong, Slater," Lisa said flatly. "It is."

▲   ▼   ▲

On Tuesday night, Kelly was a little nervous about going to work. But once again, Brad's greeting was friendly but businesslike. Maybe he'd gotten the message on Sunday that she really wasn't interested.

As she was signing in on her time card, he said, "Listen, Kelly. I know I promised you Yvonne's shift tonight. But it looks like it's going to be busy, and I'm afraid you wouldn't be able to handle it. Stick with station number one tonight."

Kelly looked at him. Was Brad punishing her, or did he really think she couldn't handle a crowd? She thought about arguing, but instead she just nodded and said, "Okay, Brad."

The night started slowly, but it picked up by seven o'clock. Kelly was starting to feel more confident at her job. It wasn't that she was crazy about waitressing. You had to keep ten different things in your head at all times, and you were constantly on your feet. But the better she got at the job, the more she was able to relax with the customers. And the more relaxed she was, the better the tips.

The night was busy, but not frantic. The time went fast. Before Kelly knew it, her shift was over. She went back to the service station, where Maria Elena was signing herself out. "I've got to run if I want to catch the ten o'clock bus," she said. "I left everything in place for tomorrow."

"Thanks," Kelly said. "Good-night, Maria Elena. See you Friday night."

Maria Elena waved good-bye, and Kelly picked up the pen to sign out. Brad appeared from the kitchen.

"Kelly? Don't sign out yet, okay? I wanted to ask you if you'd stay and set up for breakfast tomorrow. It would probably take you about an hour. I'll be shorthanded tomorrow and I could use the help. I'll pay you double time. That might make up a little for having to work the Dead Zone tonight."

Double time was good money. But Kelly hesitated.

"I'll be back in my office doing tonight's paperwork," Brad added. "The kitchen crew will be here, prepping for breakfast tomorrow."

"I'll stay," Kelly said. "Sure."

"Okay, great! Thank you. The linens are in the closet, there. It's the same setup as for lunch, only everybody gets a coffee cup. Okay?" Brad smiled at her. But it was a quick, professional smile.

"Okay," Kelly said.

She worked fast and efficiently and got the job done in an hour. Kelly put down the last coffee cup and yawned. She was beat. She walked back to the kitchen and pushed open the swinging door.

The kitchen was dark and empty. The kitchen crew had all gone home. Kelly suppressed a shiver.

It was kind of spooky in here with the lights out.

Brad opened the door behind her. "Thanks again for staying," he said. "The tables look great."

Kelly nodded. "Well, I'll be heading out," she said.

Brad moved toward her in the darkness. "You look tired," he said. He reached out and began to rub her shoulders.

Kelly hesitated. She didn't want to pull away too rudely. But she moved out from underneath his fingers within a moment. "I'm fine." She backed up toward the door to the locker room. Brad followed her. "Brad," she said quietly, "I want to go home."

"Who are you kidding?" Brad said. "You stayed. You knew I wanted to be alone with you."

"I stayed because I had a job to do," Kelly protested.

"Come on, Kelly," he said. "Don't you think it's time to stop playing hard to get? Do you want to be stuck in the Dead Zone forever?"

"Excuse me?" Kelly asked. Brad didn't repeat his comment. "Brad, I'm not playing hard to get. I'm not interested in you, period. I wish you'd understand that."

His face twisted. "What I understand is that you encouraged me. Always smiling at me—"

"I smile at people," Kelly said. "That doesn't mean I want to *date* everyone I meet. I'm friendly, that's all."

"If you don't get a little *more* friendly, you

might find yourself out of a job," Brad said.

Kelly caught her breath. "What?"

"You heard me," Brad said. He reached out and put his hands on her shoulders.

Suddenly, Kelly heard the sound of someone clearing her throat.

"Excuse me," Marie Elena said.

Brad dropped his hands from Kelly's shoulders. "What are you doing here?" he barked.

"I had to come back to make a phone call," Maria Elena said nervously. "I've been waiting for my bus for an hour. My mother should be driving home from work now, so she can pick me up."

"You know where the phone is," Brad said.

"I'd better get my stuff," Kelly said. She pushed open the door to the back hallway and hurried into the locker room.

Kelly sank onto a bench, shaking. She'd been right. Brad wasn't just being overly friendly. He was harassing her. But was he right, too? Had she encouraged him without realizing it? She *had* smiled at some of his comments. But whenever Kelly felt awkward or shy, she smiled to cover it up.

Kelly sighed shakily. This situation was just as bad as she'd thought. The question was, what should she do now?

▲　　▼　　▲

The next morning, Kelly peered eagerly through the light rain for Zack's car to pull up in the driveway. He was a few minutes late, as usual. As soon as she saw the Mustang pull into her driveway, Kelly raced out to the car and got in.

Zack didn't start the engine right away. He looked a little uneasy, and he twisted in his seat and smiled uncertainly at her.

"Uh, so how was work last night?" he asked.

"Fine," Kelly said. "But I have to talk to you about something."

"I have to talk to you, too," Zack said. "Can I go first? I've been putting this off for two days, and it's starting to choke me. Is my face purple yet?"

Kelly laughed softly. "What is it, Zack? Come on. You can tell me anything."

Zack drummed his fingers on the dashboard. "My dad asked me to do something I don't want to do. But it's really important to him. It's the first time he's asked me for a favor. I mean, aside from asking me not to leave the milk out on the counter, or not to borrow his new jacket when I'm going to work on my car. A real favor."

"Well, that's good, right?" Kelly said. "He's treating you like an adult, in a way."

"Yeah," Zack admitted. "But if this is being an adult, I'd rather stay a kid."

"What did he ask you to do?" Kelly asked curiously.

"The thing is," Zack said evasively, "he's given me a choice and everything. But I know he really, really wants me to do it. So shouldn't I help him out, even though I don't want to?"

Kelly nodded. "I think you should. I mean, he's your dad."

"Great, Kelly. I'm glad you see it that way. Because the thing he wants me to do is ask Amber Porterhouse to the Half Moon Ball." Zack said the words in a rush.

He peeked at Kelly. She was sitting there with a strange expression on her face. She wasn't angry. She wasn't sad. But she definitely wasn't happy, either.

"I won't do it if you really don't want me to," Zack said. "It's just a favor. I'd just be asking her as a friend. Amber doesn't have anyone to go with."

Kelly looked at the rain running down the windshield. She wanted to burst into tears. It wasn't that Zack was taking another girl to a dance. She understood his dilemma—sort of. It would help if she really liked Amber. But she felt as though someone had pulled the rug out from under her feet and she had gone *whomp* on hard concrete.

She couldn't look to Zack for help with Brad. He was too caught up in trying to help his father. She couldn't drag him into this. It would place him in an impossible position. Then he'd have to choose between her and his father!

"Let's just forget it," Zack said. "I can see that you're upset. I won't ask Amber."

"No, Zack," Kelly said. "I want you to. It's important to your father."

"Are you sure?" Zack asked her worriedly.

It was the hardest thing she'd ever had to do, but Kelly forced herself to smile. "I'm sure."

Zack let out a long breath. "Okay. Now, what was it you wanted to talk to me about?"

"Gee," Kelly said, forcing herself to smile. "I don't remember. Isn't that funny? It must not have been very important."

Chapter 8

▲ ▼ ▲ ▼ ▲

Later that morning, Kelly made her way to the school library. She knew that Jessie had a free period, too, and she scanned the room anxiously for her friend. Jessie was sitting on a window seat, staring out at the gray sky. Tiny rivers of rain ran down the panes.

"Hi," Jessie whispered as Kelly walked up. "Nice day, huh?"

"Pretty dismal," Kelly agreed. "Listen, are you busy studying, or can you talk?"

"I'm not busy studying," Jessie said with a sigh. "I'm busy brooding. Have a seat."

"Are things okay with Slater?" Kelly asked. "Gosh, I've been so busy with work, I feel kind of out of touch."

"Things with Slater are the usual," Jessie replied. "Meaning it's a crash-and-burn scenario. I don't want to talk about it. What's up with you?''

Kelly hesitated a minute. She'd love to confide in Jessie, but she didn't want Jessie to tell Zack the truth about Brad. Jessie was Zack's best friend, and it would be hard for her to keep a secret from him. Besides, Kelly reflected, if she told Jessie, her fiery friend would probably picket the country club. Kelly had to keep a low profile. She wanted to stop Brad, but she didn't want to wind up on the evening news. Then she'd blow Mr. Morris's chances for sure.

But during her last class, Kelly had come up with the perfect cover. "I'm doing a paper on sexual harassment," she said. "Do you know anything about it?"

"Like what about it?" Jessie asked.

"Like, if it happens to an employee, what should she do?"

"Has she been fired?" Jessie asked, frowning.

"No. And she wants to keep her job."

"Gee, Kelly, I'm not absolutely positive on this," Jessie said slowly. "I'm not a lawyer. Maybe you should talk to my mom."

"I just need a few facts to get started," Kelly said. "Didn't you go to that seminar at your women's group last month?"

"Yeah," Jessie said. "Slater wanted me to go to see *Trail of Terror* instead. We got into a huge fight." She sighed. "Okay. First of all, the employee should try to get witnesses who will say that what she says took place really did. But, usually, sexual harassment happens when other people aren't around. So the person should keep her own record. Write down *what* her boss says and *when* he said it. Date each entry. Evidence is important."

Kelly nodded slowly. *Witnesses!* She was almost positive that Maria Elena had overheard Brad on Tuesday night. She had seemed flushed and embarrassed. Unless Maria Elena thought she'd interrupted a romantic encounter between her and Brad. Kelly shuddered. That would be awful!

"Kelly? Are you okay?" Jessie asked.

"Fine," Kelly said quickly. "Is there anything else?"

Jessie shook her head. "I don't know about the legal stuff. You should definitely call my mom."

"Maybe I will," Kelly said, standing up. "Thanks, Jessie. I know things will work out with Slater."

"Sure," Jessie said glumly. "Oh, Kelly?"

Kelly stopped and looked back. "What?"

"I just thought of another piece of advice you could use for your paper."

"Great! What is it?"

Jessie gave a twisted half smile. "If all else fails, a tennis racket can always get the point across."

▲   ▼   ▲

After school, Slater tracked down Lisa in the gym, where she was practicing her splits. "Lisa, I have to talk to you," he said.

Lisa swung her legs around and did a somersault that turned into a headstand. "About what?" she asked Slater upside down.

"Me and Jessie," Slater said.

Lisa lowered her legs with a groan. "Slater, I had a pretty stress-free day today. Don't spoil it." She skipped forward a few steps and did a cartwheel that ended in a split.

Slater followed after her. "You don't understand. You got through to me. You were right. I was wrong."

Lisa looked up at him. "I have to get my hearing checked. Did you just say you were *wrong*?"

Slater nodded. "Jessie is more important than winning a stupid scavenger hunt to prove a stupid point."

"So you admit your point is stupid?" Lisa asked, doing a backbend. She frowned at him, but since she was upside down, it looked like a smile.

"Of course it's stupid!" Slater said gruffly. "You know that I said men always win just to make Jessie mad. I'm not that much of a Neanderthal."

Lisa collapsed onto the gym floor. "I wish I could tape this conversation," she said to the ceiling.

Slater crouched down next to her. "Lisa, will

you stop trying to score points off me for a second and listen? I have a solution to this whole thing: You don't want me and Jessie to break up, do you? You might not care if *I'm* miserable, but you know how we make everyone *else* miserable, too."

Lisa flipped over and looked at him. "I'm listening."

"Okay, here's the solution," Slater said. "Nobody wins."

"You'd better keep talking," Lisa said. "Because I'm not getting this."

"Here's the deal. We agree, you and me, not to win. You sabotage your team, and I'll sabotage mine. We have to be really subtle about it so that Jessie and Screech don't catch on. Just put up a few roadblocks. If you know the answer to the clue, don't say anything. Be a little slow in figuring stuff out. Things like that. Do you think you can handle it?"

"Sure," Lisa said. "But why?"

"Lisa, you know as well as I do that if I win, I'll never be able to let Jessie forget it. I'm just built that way. I can't help it."

"Then why don't you make yourself lose?" Lisa asked. "Why does Jessie have to lose, too?"

"Because she's the same way. She'd never let *me* forget it. That's why we're perfect for each other," Slater concluded with a sigh.

"I can't believe I think this is logical," Lisa said. "But I do."

"So does that mean you think it's a good idea?" Slater asked eagerly.

Lisa sat up. "I think it's a fantastic idea, Slater. I can't believe you came up with it."

"Gee, thanks," Slater said.

"I don't mean it that way," Lisa said with a soft giggle. "It's just so *devious*. Are you sure Zack didn't help you?"

Slater grinned. "Maybe Morris is rubbing off on me. So is it a deal?" He stuck out his hand.

"It's a deal," Lisa said, shaking it.

▲   ▼   ▲

After school that day, Kelly ran home to call Maria Elena. The two girls had exchanged numbers in case they needed to change shifts. She was relieved when Maria Elena answered the phone.

"Hi, it's Kelly," she said breathlessly. "From the dining room."

"Oh, hello, Kelly," Maria Elena said warmly. "It's nice to hear from you. Is there a problem with work?"

"No," Kelly said. "I mean, yes. I mean, not in the way you think. What I mean is, I'm still working Friday night. I have to talk to you about something else at work, though." Kelly knew she was babbling. But she was a little nervous.

"I see," Maria Elena said politely. She waited.

Kelly took a deep breath. "I was wondering if the other night you overheard anything that

Brad said. When you came back to use the phone, I mean."

There was a long pause. "No, I didn't," Maria Elena said. "Is there some reason you're asking?"

"Brad pretty much told me that if I didn't date him, I'd be stuck in the Dead Zone forever," Kelly said. "He also hinted that if I didn't go along, he'd fire me. You walked in just as he was saying it. You didn't hear *anything*?"

"Nothing," Maria Elena said.

"Well, you must have seen him," Kelly said. "He was standing way too close. He had his hands on my shoulders."

There was another pause. "I didn't see anything, Kelly," Maria Elena said. "I was coming from light to dark. My eyes hadn't adjusted."

Kelly tapped her fingers on the phone. She had a feeling Maria Elena was lying. But she couldn't force the girl to talk. "Please, Maria Elena," she said quietly. "I need help. If we stick together, we won't lose our jobs."

This time, the pause stretched out for long seconds. "I'm sorry, Kelly," Maria Elena said. "I didn't see or hear anything. I'm really sorry."

There was a soft click in Kelly's ear. Maria Elena had hung up.

▲   ▼   ▲

Lisa switched off her bedside light and snuggled down under the covers. She heaved a happy sigh. Today, she had agreed to do a good deed. She was helping her friend Jessie keep the guy she loved. Jessie would never know that Lisa had given up a chance at two hundred and fifty dollars for her friend's happiness. Lisa tried not to think of all the cute outfits two hundred and fifty dollars could buy.

Lisa turned over. Jessie and Slater's relationship was worth it. Jessie might be disappointed about not winning, but it wouldn't last. Once she and Slater were together again, Jessie would realize that her relationship was more important.

Funny how she'd gotten through to Slater today. Usually, his head was as hard as granite. Lisa must have been really persuasive. Maybe she should join the debating team. Vincent Tolson was on it, and he was kind of cute.

Lisa's thoughts started to jumble together. Vincent Tolson . . . scavenger hunt . . . sardines . . . backbends . . . *Maybe Morris has rubbed off on me*. . . . Scams . . .

Lisa's eyes flew open. "Scams?" she asked out loud. Was her subconscious trying to tell her something?

What if Slater's whole plan had been a scam?

Lisa sat up and switched on the light. She had to think. What if Slater had tricked her? What if *he* wasn't going to slow down his team, but he wanted Lisa to slow down Jessie? It was a perfect plan if he wanted to win.

It *had* been weird when Slater admitted he was wrong. He *never* admitted he was wrong. And he'd said that his point that men were smarter than women was stupid! Slater would *never* admit that! He *was* a Neanderthal.

Lisa frowned. Slater had seemed really sincere, though. She knew how much Jessie meant to him. She didn't think he would sucker her like that. That was just too mean, even for someone whose girlfriend had given him a black eye.

Then, again, he had seemed pretty angry about the black eye. . . .

Lisa flopped back in bed, exasperated. Slater could have been lying. He could have been telling the truth. If she sabotaged the team on Saturday and Slater won, it would be her fault. And if she *didn't* sabotage the team, Jessie and Slater might break up. And that would be her fault! Not to mention that Slater would hate her for letting him down.

Lisa put the pillow over her head and moaned. What was she going to do?

Chapter 9

▲ ▼ ▲ ▼ ▲

The next morning, Kelly woke up feeling depressed. She wanted to stay in bed all day. She wanted to stay in bed for the next *three* days, then her mother would be home. Then her mother could call Brad and tell him that he was a mean person and she wouldn't let Kelly work for him anymore. Kelly smiled faintly. Sometimes, she just wanted to be a little kid again.

She knew Kerry or Kirby wouldn't bring her meals for the next three days, so she'd probably starve. Kelly decided to get up. She dressed slowly and shuffled downstairs to eat a bowl of cereal before it was time to leave for school.

While she was munching on her raisin flakes, her brother Kerry came in. He grabbed an apple and gave her a glance. "What's up, squirt? If you don't watch out, your chin is going to land in your cereal."

"Just tired," Kelly mumbled. She couldn't confide in her breezy brother Kerry. She couldn't tell him what she was thinking. She couldn't say that she hadn't meant to lead Brad on. She couldn't say that she was scared that the whole thing was all her fault.

Kerry bit into his apple. "Working two jobs is tough, huh?"

"The worst," Kelly said. She was working at the Yogurt 4-U after school today. Actually, she was almost looking forward to Gus's gruffness. At least she knew where she stood with Gus.

"This acting thing must be pretty important to you," Kerry said. "Little did I know I was living with a future Julia Roberts."

"We'll see," Kelly said. Her spoon clattered in her empty bowl, and she got up to put her dishes into the sink. She began to rinse them out.

"It's funny, too," Kerry said. "You're the last person I'd expect to get bitten by the acting bug."

"Why is that, Kerry?" Kelly asked wearily. She knew a wisecrack was coming.

Kerry shrugged. "I just can't imagine you in that world. Remember Alison Sperry, that actress I dated? She always told me about all the sharks in Hollywood. Actresses have to be tough. You have to know how to stand up for yourself. I mean, you probably have talent, since you're *my* sister, and you're not even bad looking, so I guess it could happen for you. Just don't let 'em get to you. And if they do, just come and get me."

He ambled out, munching on his apple. Kelly froze, the warm water running over her fingers. Kerry had surprised her. He hadn't made fun of her. He'd said something so true, she couldn't even move for a minute. It was like she'd been peering in a dusty mirror, and he'd come along with glass cleaner.

She *didn't* know how to stand up for herself. Not really. She'd always had someone, her brothers or her parents or Zack or Jessie, to do it for her. Nobody had ever said that to her so bluntly. But it was true.

Maybe it was because all of her life, people had told her she was pretty. As a result, she didn't have the same spunk someone like Jessie or Lisa had. They were both pretty girls now, but they'd each gone through an awkward stage when they were younger. In the space of a summer, Jessie had shot up to her present height. Now she was a knock-out with long legs, but at eleven, she'd looked like a giraffe. Lisa hadn't grown at all, but she had been a little plump. She'd lost weight and toned up the summer she was fourteen, and she'd been a dating queen ever since.

But during their awkward stages, Jessie and Lisa had had to learn how to stand up for them-selves when someone teased them. Jessie had developed wit and courage. Lisa had learned to trust in her own sure intuition and to call a jerk a jerk without worrying about looking mean or foolish.

Kelly had never learned those things. First of all, she'd never had an awkward stage. It seemed like one week, she was an active tomboy, and the next, she was getting whistles at the beach. So she'd never had to rely on something other than her looks. And there were always plenty of guys around to stand up for her. Her boyfriend in seventh grade, Tony Annuncio, had gotten her money back when the ice-cream vendor cheated her. Jessie had spoken up for her when her eighth-grade teacher, Mrs. Cale, had wrongly accused her of cheating. And Zack—well, Zack had always been there to watch out for her. Even Kerry, who usually teased her unmercifully, had just offered to run interference for her.

She was lucky to have such good friends and family, Kelly thought, turning off the water. But just because they kept offering to help her, did that mean she had to accept? At this rate, she'd never learn to stand up for herself.

Kelly dried her hands purposefully. It was time to stop smiling and get serious. It was time to fight back.

But where to start? Kelly sank down at the breakfast table, thinking hard. How would *Jessie* handle the situation with Brad? she asked herself.

The answer came with swift sureness.

She wouldn't blame herself.

None of this was her fault. Brad was the one who'd turned out the lights and stood too close. He was the one who'd blocked the door to his office. He was the one who'd offered her a better station and then taken it away. And no matter what he said, she hadn't encouraged him! Even if he *had* misread her signals, Kelly realized, she still didn't deserve to be treated that way.

She was afraid to go to work. She was afraid to be trapped alone with Brad. That just wasn't right!

Her mother wasn't here. Maria Elena wouldn't help her. She couldn't ask for Zack's help. This was *her* problem. She had to solve it herself, and she had to stop thinking that someone else would. Brad wasn't going to disappear. If she wanted to keep her job, she'd have to deal with him. She'd have to be ready for him on Friday.

Kelly reached for the memo pad her mother kept on the kitchen table for the grocery list. She went back in her mind to her very first day at work. Then she began to write. She wasn't going to be Brad's victim anymore.

▲   ▼   ▲

On Friday night, Zack stopped by Amber Porterhouse's mansion on Grandview Lane. The house was a huge, modern structure overlooking the Pacific way below. It was definitely impressive, but

Zack would rather be anywhere but there.

Amber had called and suggested he drop by so that he'd know where to pick her up on Saturday night. She didn't want him to be late for the ball. She also wanted to show him the exact shade of her dress so that he'd know what kind of flowers to get her. The reason seemed pretty bogus to Zack, but Amber definitely seemed to be a bit of a control freak. He didn't really blame her boyfriend for dumping her.

Amber opened the door and smiled at him. "Zack! You're five minutes late."

"I took a wrong turn," Zack said, stepping into the hallway. It was a huge space with a skylight in the ceiling. Moonlight filtered down to illuminate pots of blooming pink plants.

"Well, it's lucky I set up this meeting, isn't it," Amber said. She led the way across the hall to double walnut doors. She opened them, and Zack found himself in a living room as big as a football field. There were three sets of couches sprinkled around, and a long table piled with the latest issue of every magazine Zack had ever seen.

"I guess so," he said, looking around. A huge picture window at the end of the room overlooked the dark ocean.

"Let me show you the swatch of my dress," Amber said. "It's more of an apricot than a pink, you see. So I'd like to get flowers in the pinky orange range, rather than the pinky red. What do you think?"

"The pinky orange, for sure," Zack said.

"Now, I don't want us to be the first ones there," Amber said, catching her lower lip in her teeth and thinking hard. "I guess you should pick me up between seven-ten and seven-fourteen."

"Are you sure we shouldn't make that seven-o-nine?" Zack asked sarcastically.

She frowned. "Good point."

Dad, I love you, Zack thought. *But if you ask me to take this girl out again, I'll kill myself.*

"So, now that we have that settled, what's new?" Amber said. She patted a spot next to her on a cream-colored couch.

Zack perched on the arm of the couch. "Oh, I heard a funny thing the other day," he said.

Amber brightened. "Yes?"

"You know my girlfriend, Kelly?"

Amber frowned. "Y-ees?"

"Well, it turns out that your brother, Brad, is her boss!"

Amber nodded slowly. "I heard that," she said. "But I thought I shouldn't bring it up."

"Why not?" Zack asked.

Amber bit her lip. "Well, because I don't know how much longer she'll be there, Zack. I'm sorry. Brad says she's just not a very good waitress."

"What are you talking about?" Zack asked. "She's doing fine."

"I guess she's putting up a front. But Brad says she's pretty hopeless. Plus—oh, gosh, I *really* don't want to tell you this—but Brad says she's a terrible flirt. She flirts with all the customers. Not to mention Brad."

Zack laughed. "Kelly? No way. She's just friendly."

"No, really, Zack. I don't know how long you guys have been going out or anything, but—"

"I've known Kelly all my life," Zack said steadily. He was starting to get annoyed.

"Well, Brad says that she really came on to him. And Brad doesn't lie," Amber said.

"Well, Kelly doesn't lie, either," Zack said. "And she's not a flirt." He stood up angrily. "And I don't think it's very nice of you and your brother to spread stories about her."

"We're not spreading *stories*, for heaven's sake," Amber said, smoothing her skirt. "But we *do* have friends at the club. You're a new member, Zack. I'm just giving you a word to the wise. You should be careful who you associate with. You know, Daddy thinks that your father is the best thing since lemon Perrier. You wouldn't want Daddy to think your father wasn't strictly top drawer, would you? So if your girlfriend is a waitress ..." Amber shrugged. "Draw your own conclusions, okay?"

"I'd be glad to," Zack said menacingly. "Only I don't think you'd like to hear them."

"Hey, don't get hostile," Amber said. "I'm just warning you. Daddy's always saying how the apple doesn't fall far from the tree."

Zack sniffed the air. "Oh. Is that why I smell something rotten? I didn't realize it was *apples*."

Amber's eyes flashed. "Well, you don't have to get *nasty*."

"Excuse me," Zack said. "It seemed to be the way the conversation was going. I was just following along." He started toward the door.

"Where are you going?" Amber wailed. "What about tomorrow night?"

Zack stopped. "Sorry, Amber. You're going to have to pick out your pinky red flowers by yourself."

"Pinky *orange*!" Amber flung after him just as he slammed the front door.

Zack stood in the darkness, thinking about what Amber had said. He didn't believe Brad's stories for a minute, so what did that say about Brad?

He's kind of weird, Kelly had said. *He's always complimenting me*. And hadn't she said that when she'd turned him down for a date, he'd gotten angry? That definitely was *not* cool behavior.

And what had Zack said? He'd told her she was overreacting. *Brad sounds like a normal guy to me. Give the guy a break.*

Zack wanted to kick himself. What kind of a boyfriend *was* he? Kelly had been worried and scared, and he'd told her she was imagining things!

Zack didn't know what was going on. But he did know that something was wrong. Something was very, very wrong.

▲   ▼   ▲

Kelly signed herself out on her time card. Her shift had flown by. It was fish fry night, and she'd been carrying heavy platters full of shrimp and catfish and french fries all night long. She'd really raked in the tips, even in the Dead Zone.

She turned around and almost bumped into Brad. "Oh, sorry," she said quickly, starting off.

"Whoa, what's the rush, sweetie?" Brad asked.

Kelly swung around. "I'd prefer it if you didn't call me that, Brad. It makes me uncomfortable."

"It's an endearment, Kelly," Brad said. "A compliment to your beauty and grace. Lighten up. So what do you have planned for this evening? I hope it isn't a date with your boyfriend."

"Why is that?" Kelly asked.

"Because he's with my sister, Amber," Brad said smugly. "So you don't have one good reason not to go out with me."

"Try this one," Kelly said. "I'd rather chew nails."

Brad frowned. "I don't like that, Kelly. I don't like that at all."

"You know what, Brad?" Kelly asked. "I

really don't care. I've tried to let you know in a polite way that I don't want to go out with you, but you say I'm encouraging you. So maybe you'll get the point if I'm rude."

Brad held up his hands. "Whoa. I'm just trying to get along with you. I guess you *like* the Dead Zone, huh? You don't want to advance here."

Kelly looked around and lowered her voice. "Brad, I've tried to tell you over the past week that your behavior is insulting, inappropriate, and wrong. Now I'm telling you that if you don't stop, I'll file charges against you. You've used your power to try to make me go out with you. That qualifies as sexual harassment. I have documentation, and I'll use it." She stopped, her face flushed. She'd gotten it out!

Brad's jaw dropped. "You can't do that," he said.

"Try me," Kelly said. She met his gaze without blinking. "But if you treat me from now on in a professional manner, nobody has to know."

"Don't you threaten me," Brad said in a high-pitched voice. His face was bright red. "Nobody threatens me."

"I guess there's a first time for everything," Kelly said coolly. Jessie couldn't have done it better, she was sure.

She walked off toward the ladies' room. She felt a little shaky, but surprisingly okay. If this was how standing up for herself felt, it felt pretty good. She'd gotten angry, but she'd stayed in control. She'd told Brad what she thought, and the floor hadn't opened up and swallowed her.

In the ladies' room, Kelly splashed cool water on her face. She took several deep breaths and then smiled at herself in the mirror. It was over, she told herself. Brad would *have* to behave professionally now. He'd really looked scared.

She went down the hall to the locker room and pushed open the door. She nearly jumped three feet in the air when she saw Brad standing by her open locker. He'd used his master key!

Kelly's heart fell in dread. He was holding the memo pad she'd put in her purse. The one that detailed every time he'd made a threatening or inappropriate remark.

He was smiling as he tapped it against his palm. "Did you really think you would get away with this pack of lies?"

"They're not lies," Kelly said. "And you know it."

He took a step toward her. "I know that from the first day you started working here, you came on to me. Just because I asked you to work late and there was a mix-up with the busboys, you held a grudge."

"You deliberately didn't assign Armand to my tables!" Kelly cried.

He shook his head sadly. "That's not true, Kelly. And how are you going to prove it, anyway? You think that by writing down lies, it makes them *true*?"

"They *are* true," Kelly said. She felt tears burn her eyes, but she willed them not to fall. She wouldn't let Brad make her cry. She wouldn't!

Brad slipped the memo pad into his pocket. "It's your word against mine, Kelly. And I see a sloppy, disorganized waitress who's blaming her lack of skill on her boss. I can't have you destroying the morale of my staff. You're fired. I've made out your last paycheck, including tonight's wages. Don't come back here ever again."

He held out the paycheck. Kelly wanted to rip it up right in front of him, but she wouldn't give him the satisfaction. She looked at it and saw immediately that he hadn't paid her for her overtime.

"My overtime," she said. "We had an agreement. You didn't pay me for it."

Brad smirked. "So sue me," he said, and walked out.

Chapter 10

▲ ▼ ▲ ▼ ▲

Zack found his father in his study, going over some business plans. He looked up eagerly when he saw Zack.

"Your mother said you went over to see Amber. How did it go?"

"Not too good, Dad," Zack said.

Mr. Morris frowned. "Don't tell me you're not going to the Half Moon Ball together."

"Okay, Dad," Zack said. "I won't tell you if you don't want me to."

Mr. Morris smacked his hand down on his papers. One of them blew away and skated along the floor. "Not again, Zack!" he said. "Don't tell me you messed up again!"

Zack suddenly flashed back to himself at six, and ten, and fourteen, standing in this very same spot and hearing the same words. No wonder he spent so much time in Mr. Belding's office. There, he stood in the very same position, hearing the very same words. It was just like home.

"Dad, can I explain?"

"You always have an *explanation*, Zack," his father said, running his hands through his hair in exasperation.

"First of all, I don't think it's fair that you tied a business deal to my social life," Zack said. He saw his father give a start, a strange expression on his face. "I agreed to take out Mr. Porterhouse's daughter because I wanted to help you out. But I found out tonight that those perfect Porterhouse kids are pretty rotten. They're deliberately hurting Kelly, and I'm not going to stand for that."

Zack paused. He kept his eyes on his father. He didn't shift his feet or make a joke. This was a very important conversation, he realized. He was letting his father know that *he* had limits, too.

"I know that my relationship with Kelly is probably kid stuff to you," Zack said. "We're young and all that. But I've loved her all my life, Dad. And I can't hurt her. I won't hurt her. Not even for you," he said firmly.

Mr. Morris didn't say anything for a while. He stared at the floor. He was probably trying to calm himself so he wouldn't explode. Zack waited for the blast. The lecture, the grounding, the You-can't-use-the-car-for-a-week routine. But he didn't care. For the first time, standing in his father's study, he didn't feel miserable or guilty. He felt just fine.

Mr. Morris cleared his throat. "I haven't said anything yet, Zack, because I don't know what to say. I'm ashamed of myself, actually. You were right on the money." He laughed a harsh laugh. "I chose the right phrase. *Money.* I don't have it, and I need it badly. And because of that, I asked you to do something I shouldn't have. You're absolutely right."

"I am?" Zack asked. "I mean, you think I am?"

"Thank you for helping me see the light," Mr. Morris said. "Your mother tried to tell me. She isn't very happy with me right now. She found out that I asked you to bring Amber to the dance instead of Kelly. Why do you think I'm sitting in the study on a Friday night?" He grinned sheepishly.

Zack grinned back. "It's okay, Dad," he said. "We all know how important starting this company is to you. And we all want you to have it. You didn't order me to take Amber out. You *asked* me."

"But I asked you in a way you couldn't possibly refuse," his dad said. "As you would say, that stinks. And by the way, I don't see your relationship with Kelly as 'kid stuff.' I'm truly sorry she got hurt. I love her, too. She's a part of the family. I'll apologize to her when I see her."

If you see her again, Zack thought. *Because*

*after the way I treated her, she might be gone
forever. And I wouldn't blame her a bit.*

"So are we square now?" his father asked.
"Do you forgive me?"

"Forgive *you*? That's a switch," Zack said.
"Of course I do, Dad."

His father stood up. "Great. Now, will you do
me a favor and get me out of the doghouse with
your mom?"

Zack grinned. "Sure."

Mr. Morris started toward the door. But then
he did a strange thing. He walked back to the spot
where Zack always stood to get his punishment.
And then he hugged his son.

▲   ▼   ▲

Kelly drove back home and started the hot
water running in the tub while she ran downstairs
for a soda. She was determined to put the whole
incident with Brad out of her mind. She'd done
everything she could. She'd never dreamed Brad
would break into her locker. She'd lost, but she'd
said what she needed to, and it was okay. She'd just
have to get another job.

The only trouble was, she'd been to every
place she could think of before trying the country
club. Everyone had wanted major waitressing experience. Brad was the only one to take a chance on
her. And now she knew why!

At least she had her paycheck. She could put

it toward the cost of the seminar. Maybe Gus would give her a couple of more nights at the Yogurt 4-U. Kelly dug into her purse. She'd forgotten the exact amount of the check.

Kelly searched through her purse, then turned it upside down. Her paycheck was missing!

Kelly frowned. What could have happened? She remembered slipping it into her pocket after Brad left the locker room. Then she . . .

Then she'd taken off her uniform and had left it in the locker with her paycheck in the pocket!

Kelly looked at her watch. It wasn't too late. Brad was probably gone by now. And what could he do to her? He wasn't her boss anymore!

Kelly turned off the tap in the bathroom, grabbed her purse, and flew out the door. There was no traffic, and she made it to the club in fifteen minutes. No one in the lobby noticed her as she made her way toward the dining room. She went past the door marked EMPLOYEES ONLY and down the short hall.

Kelly heaved a sigh of relief when she saw that the locker room was dark and empty. She quickly opened her locker and reached into the pocket of the uniform. Her paycheck was still there, thank goodness!

She slipped it into her purse and started out into the hall. But as she started back toward the lobby, she heard voices. Kelly stopped. It was Brad.

She tiptoed closer to the door that led to the kitchen.

"Thanks again for staying late, Maria Elena," Brad said. "Now we'll have an easy time at breakfast tomorrow."

"Don't mention it, Mr. Porterhouse."

"Hey—what's this 'Mr. Porterhouse' all of a sudden? You know we're informal around here."

"Brad," Maria Elena said reluctantly.

"Ooo, I like the way you say my name. Say it again."

"Really, I have to go—"

"Say it, Maria Elena."

"Brad," she whispered.

"That's nice. Listen, I was wondering. Can you stay late Saturday, too? We're going to be super busy because of the Half Moon Ball."

"Saturday? I don't think so."

"Gee, Maria Elena," Brad said in a wounded voice. "I hope that I'm not seeing an attitude problem developing here. We all have to pitch in. Do you want to get demoted to the Dead Zone, where the naughty waitresses go? Or get fired? I'd hate to do that. You're my favorite waitress."

There was a bump on the other side of the door to the kitchen. Kelly's hands were shaking. She knew Brad had Maria Elena backed up against it. What should she do?

Kelly started toward the door, but before she

could reach it, Maria Elena said, "I'll see you Saturday, Brad. I really have to go now."

Kelly melted back around a corner as Maria Elena came out of the door, her face flushed and her eyes bright with tears. For a second, Kelly saw Brad's smug face before the door swung shut again. Maria Elena ran inside the ladies' locker room.

Kelly pushed open the door. Maria Elena was huddled on a bench, crying. Kelly sat next to her.

"I heard some of what happened," Kelly said sympathetically. "I'm sorry."

"Oh, Kelly," Maria Elena said, trying to dry her eyes with a napkin from the dining room. "It's me who's sorry. I knew what Brad was doing to you. I *did* overhear him that night. And even before that, I had my suspicions. That's why I came to his office that night when you were in there."

"Thanks," Kelly said.

"Don't thank me," Maria Elena said. "It took me a while to figure out what was going on. I think maybe he came on to Yvonne, too. I think she even went out with him. That's why he bumped me off the good station and gave it to her. Then when I tried to talk to him about rotating the stations, he told me it was sour grapes." Maria Elena sighed. "I'm really sorry, Kelly. I should have told you all this. But . . ."

"I understand," Kelly said. "You were afraid of losing your job. It's okay."

Maria Elena sighed. "It wasn't just that," she murmured. "My mother is an undocumented worker, and Brad found out. He kept making references to her to let me know that he'd tell."

"He's been blackmailing you!" Kelly exclaimed. "That weasel!"

Maria Elena nodded. "What am I going to do?" she whispered. "That little weasel has power. He'll always win."

Kelly's lips pressed together determinedly. Brad was picking on someone more vulnerable than she was. That was the way he operated. She wasn't going to let him get away with it!

"No, he won't," Kelly said firmly. "Not this time. We can fight him, Maria Elena. We've got to face him down."

Maria Elena hesitated. "I don't know, Kelly. What can we do? I can't do anything legally. I don't want to get my mother in trouble."

Kelly bit her lip. "I'll think of something," she promised.

Suddenly, she heard a voice behind her. "And I'll help."

Kelly turned. It was Zack!

"What are you doing here?" she breathed. "Maria Elena, this is my boyfriend, Zack Morris."

Zack said hello to Maria Elena. Then he looked at Kelly. "I'd get down on my knees, but this floor doesn't look too clean." He smiled uncertainly. "I came to say I'm sorry, Kelly. I realized you were trying to tell me something about Brad, and I was too stupid to hear it. I meant what I said. I want to help. That is, if you'll let me."

"What about your father?" Kelly asked.

Zack shrugged. "He'll deal."

"Or he *won't* deal," Kelly said ruefully. "With Mr. Porterhouse, that is."

Maria Elena looked at Kelly. "Your boyfriend's father knows Brad's father?"

Kelly nodded. "He wants to do a big deal with Nathan Porterhouse."

"And exposing Brad would mean the deal might fall through," Maria Elena said slowly.

"I would hope Mr. Porterhouse wouldn't be that vindictive," Zack said. "I'm willing to take the chance."

Maria Elena stood up slowly. "So you are taking a big risk, too," she said to Zack. "The least I can do is join you."

"Oh, Maria Elena, I'm so glad," Kelly said, jumping up. "We can do it, I know we can. We can't let Brad do this to other girls. We have to stop him. We have to make him realize that what he's doing is wrong."

The three of them looked at each other. "Now we just have to figure out how," Zack said.

▲   ▼   ▲

On Saturday morning, Lisa dreamed about a tugboat pulling away from a pier in the rain. Slater was on it, while onshore, Jessie cried and waved. Slater stood, unmoving and unsmiling, while the deep blare of the tugboat's horn drowned out the sound of Jessie's tears.

Honk. Honk. Honk.

Lisa sat up in bed. The honk was coming from outside her window. Sleepily, she climbed out of bed and pushed back the curtains. She almost expected to see a tugboat in her driveway, but, instead, it was Jessie's little blue Toyota. Jessie was standing beside it, her hand on the horn.

"Please," Lisa begged, "if you value our friendship, don't hit that horn again."

"Hey, sleepyhead," Jessie said. "Wake up. It's time to get moving."

"What are you talking about?" Lisa asked, yawning. "The sun is barely even up."

"It's seven o'clock," Jessie informed her.

"We're not supposed to be at the park until ten," Lisa said.

"But we need a good parking space," Jessie said. "It's strategy. We have to be able to pull out without waiting behind a bunch of other cars. So get moving."

"Girl, you know I don't step a foot out of this house without a shower," Lisa told her firmly. "I'll only be a few minutes. Go around to the back door and I'll let you into the kitchen. My mom probably left some doughnuts on the table before she left for the hospital."

Jessie was only on her second cinnamon roll when Lisa hurried downstairs, dressed for action in an apricot safari suit. She grabbed a doughnut and an apple and ate breakfast on the way downtown.

Jessie got the parking space she wanted, and the two girls settled in to wait on the steps of the city hall. The little park was completely empty.

"Nobody here but us pigeons," Lisa said, tossing a crumb to one of the fat birds.

"We did the right thing," Jessie said. "You'll see. Wait until Slater gets here and he can't park."

Slowly, the park began to fill with the other contestants. Slater showed up at nine fifty-nine. He double-parked at the edge of the park and sauntered over with Screech.

"That's illegal, you know," Jessie said, her hazel eyes flashing.

"Arrest me, momma," Slater answered with a grin. He held out his wrists.

Jessie couldn't help smiling. "Why bother? You're incorrigible."

Mr. Frederick appeared and held the new clues aloft. He told them good luck as volunteers handed out the envelopes to each team. Then, at his signal, everyone tore open their envelopes and quickly scanned the clues.

"Let's do it differently this time," Jessie said in an undertone to Lisa. "We'll start with the easiest clues and leave the hardest for last."

"Good thinking," Lisa said. She peeked at Slater. He was reading the clues rapidly and conferring with Screech. He didn't *look* like someone who was planning to lose.

Jessie read a clue out loud to Lisa. "DON'T GO BONKERS—U CAN REPLACE THE O IF YOU BRING BACK FLOWERS FROM THE FIELD. Wow," Jessie said. "This one makes no sense at all. Maybe we should leave it for now."

Lisa frowned at the paper. " 'U can replace the O? It sounds like a Prince song."

Jessie giggled. "Do you think Damon Frederick is a fan?"

"Wait a second," Lisa said. "Maybe the clue is telling us what to do."

"What do you mean, Lisa?" Jessie asked eagerly.

"I'm talking about the letters," Lisa explained. "If you replace the *u*'s with *o*'s, what do you get?"

"Dun't gu bunkers," Jessie said. "Sounds like Norwegian for 'chill out.' "

Lisa laughed. "But we're only supposed to replace *one* o. The only word that makes sense at all is bunkers. Isn't a bunker some kind of a military thing?"

"It's an underground fortification, I think," Jessie said. Suddenly, she snapped her fingers. "Got it." She leaned in closer. "You know Fort

Fielding, don't you? It's on the coast about twenty minutes south of town. That's where the military stored weapons during World War II. They built these huge bunkers right into the hills. They were also used as lookouts for Japanese submarines. It's a state park now."

"Of course," Lisa breathed. "I've been there. It's where people go hang gliding. And at this time of year, all the ice plants will be in bloom. Flowers from the field. That's what we have to bring back!"

"Let's go," Jessie murmured. "The car is around the corner, so Slater won't even see us."

Lisa frowned as she followed Jessie's purposeful stride. She'd gotten a little carried away just then and forgotten that she was supposed to slow things up. But *was* she going to slow things up? She still wasn't sure if Slater was trying to trick her. If he was, she would blow the whole contest. Not to mention the five hundred dollars for her and Jessie.

Lisa sighed, remembering her dream. If she *did* do her best to win the contest, Jessie would end up on some pier, crying her eyes out as Slater pulled away on a tugboat.

It was an impossible decision. But sometime today, Lisa would have to make it. And she'd better be right!

Chapter 11

▲ ▼ ▲ ▼ ▲

By three o'clock Saturday afternoon, Lisa and Jessie had run through the entire list of clues except one and gotten them all. They had collected flowers from Fort Fielding and a copy of a land grant from the hall of records. They had bought a replica of the statue of Juan Domenica Corazon at the park and had copied the names of the soldiers from Palisades who died in World War I off the war memorial. They had a shopping bag full of items to prove how hard they'd worked that day.

All the while she was checking off clues and racing through Palisades, Lisa was agonizing over her dilemma. She just couldn't decide what to do!

But even if she *could* decide, she'd still have a problem. Jessie was hot. She was a lean, mean scavenger-hunt machine. She figured out the answers to clues almost before Lisa had finished reading them.

She puzzled out directions. She made every green light in town, and she never ran out of gas. Lisa was exhausted!

"If you don't slow down, girlfriend, I'm going to have circles under my eyes at the ball tonight," Lisa grumbled as Jessie chewed on her pen and stared at the final clue.

"We only have one more clue, Lisa," Jessie said excitedly. "Just one more! Isn't it fantastic? We're going to be the first ones done. And if we've got the right answers, we'll win! I can't wait to see Slater's face when our names are announced tonight."

Lisa sighed. Jessie was so intent on beating her boyfriend, she wasn't thinking of the consequences. That's what Slater had been afraid of. He must have been on the level, Lisa realized. He wouldn't have tricked her. Even Zack wouldn't stoop that low. And despite Slater's big mouth, he had the mushiest heart in the world. Especially when it came to Jessie.

"Couldn't we do something really radical now, like have lunch?" Lisa suggested.

"Are you crazy?" Jessie said. "We don't have time."

"Well, I can't figure this clue out," Lisa said. "It's a doozy." She read it out loud. "BRING BACK SOME DARK GRAINS OF PROOF FROM FRANK'S FIRST STOP. No wonder we left it for last. Who's Frank? What's his first stop? Is he a bus driver? Are we supposed to know the names of every bus driver in Palisades? I never even *take* the bus."

"I don't think it's a bus driver, Lisa," Jessie said. "And what are dark grains of proof? Dark grains make me think of wild rice. Maybe Frank is Uncle Ben's brother."

"I keep thinking of sand," Lisa said. "But that's silly. Sand is white. Or beige, really. Actually, I'd call it more of an ecru. . . ."

"There's black sand, too," Jessie said. "Like the sand at Midnight Cove." Suddenly, Jessie grabbed Lisa's arm. "That's it!"

"What? Hey, watch my arm. My dress for tonight is sleeveless," Lisa said.

"Lisa, don't you get it?" Jessie asked, dropping her arm. "Frank is a Francis!"

"Who's Francis?" Lisa asked doubtfully. "Another bus driver?"

"*Sir* Francis," Jessie explained.

"A *royal* bus driver?" Lisa shook her head. "That's wild."

"Sir Francis Drake, you bonehead," Jessie said. "Don't you remember Mr. Loomis telling us about him? He was a famous British explorer back in the sixteenth century. He came ashore in Palisades. He was looking for fresh water."

"I remember Drake," Lisa asked. "But after he had a drink, didn't he go right to San Francisco like most of the tourists?"

Jessie laughed. "Right. But he and his men anchored in *Midnight Cove*."

"So we're supposed to bring back some sand from the cove," Lisa said. "That's the dark grains."

"Exactly," Jessie said. "And then we're going to win!" She leaned over to turn on the ignition.

"Where is Midnight Cove, anyway?" Lisa asked. "I think I was there when I was a kid."

Jessie paused. "I'm not sure," she said. "I think it's north of town."

"I thought it was south," Lisa said. Suddenly, she had an idea. If she was going to prevent Jessie from winning, this was her only chance.

"We'd better look at the map," Jessie said. "We have to hurry!"

"I have an idea," Lisa said. "Let me drive. You direct me. You're much better at map reading than I am. If I gave directions, we'd end up in San Diego."

"That's for sure," Jessie said with a laugh.

Jessie and Lisa got out of the car and ran around it to switch sides. Lisa headed for the coast road while Jessie unfolded the map. Then, following Jessie's careful directions, she drove north for several miles.

Jessie leaned forward, peering across the road. "Slow down, Lisa. The entrance to the cove might not be marked. And I think it's a dirt road. It's the first turn after Sunset Lane, and we just passed that road."

Lisa took her foot off the gas.

"Not *that* slow," Jessie complained. "We won't get there until next Thursday."

Lisa speeded up a bit. How was she going to foil this enterprise? Jessie was keen as a hawk.

"There it is!" Jessie cried. "Make a left onto that dirt road up ahead."

Lisa turned. It was now or never. The road was hard-packed dirt, but there was a shoulder of soft sand running alongside. Lisa turned the wheel and drove right onto it. The wheels spun crazily, and the car stalled.

"Lisa! What are you doing?" Jessie cried. "We're stuck!"

"Gosh, I'm so sorry," Lisa said. "I don't know how that could have happened."

"I'll see if I can push us out," Jessie said. She got out of the car and leaned against the rear bumper. "Okay, step on the gas."

Lisa stepped on the gas. The tires whined and spun wildly. Sand flew out into Jessie's face.

"Stop!" Jessie said, wiping at her streaming eyes. "You're only digging in deeper. I'll try to find something to put under the wheels."

Just then, they heard the sound of a car engine.

"Someone's coming!" Jessie said excitedly. "They can help push us out."

She turned expectantly. Slater's Chevy came barreling down the road, leaving a trail of dust. He honked several times, and he and Screech yelled and waved triumphantly.

"They didn't stop to help!" Jessie said, coughing from the dust.

"No, they didn't," Lisa said slowly.

"Now they're going straight to the cove!" Jessie cried. "They'll get the sand before us!"

"They sure will," Lisa said. "That snake! That two-timing, double-crossing piece of slime!"

"Calm down, Lisa," Jessie said. "You're beginning to sound like me."

"You don't understand," Lisa said, almost in tears. "I fell for Slater's act big time. And now he and Screech are going to win! Oh, Jessie, I'm so sorry. It's just that you were on the pier, and he was on the tugboat, and . . . I guess we're sunk," Lisa concluded.

Jessie looked at her curiously. "What act? What tugboat? And why are you sorry?"

Quickly, Lisa filled Jessie in on her conversation with Slater. Jessie's expression got more and more furious as the story unfolded.

"He's worse than a snake!" Jessie said. "He's . . . he's . . . There isn't a word invented yet for what he is! How could you fall for that line, Lisa?"

"*You* fall for his lines," Lisa pointed out, sniffing.

Jessie began to pace back and forth. "I'm not going to let him get away with this. I'm going to fix his wagon." She stopped. "Hey, wait a second. That's exactly what I'm going to do."

"What are you thinking, girl?" Lisa asked. "You look awfully devious. I like it."

"See if you can get us out of this," Jessie said, waving at the car. "Find some of those big surfers you love to drool over and act helpless. I'll be right back."

▲   ▼   ▲

On the beach at Midnight Cove, Screech was chortling as he filled a plastic cup with sand. "This is it, Slater!" he said. "We're going to win! You were right. The girls didn't stand a chance."

"Right," Slater said. He thought worriedly about Jessie. It would have looked too weird if he'd helped the girls get their car unstuck. Besides, it might have been part of Lisa's plan. He hoped some able-bodied weight lifters would happen along. But not too quickly. He didn't want Jessie to win after all the trouble he went to!

Screech turned and looked at him, his eyes shining. "You know what? I've never won anything. Belinda Towser beats me out at the science fair every year. I buy five books of raffle tickets and never win a thing. I've come in last at every spelling bee since grade school. This feels really great. This is the best day of my life!"

"That's great, Screech," Slater said. Now he really felt guilty. He hadn't thought that winning meant that much to Screech. But it was too late to back out. He'd already drained most of the water from his car radiator. It would overheat halfway back to Palisades.

"I just wish I had my video camera to record this for posterity. For the first time in my life, I'll get some glory," Screech said. "Thanks, buddy. It's all because of you. You made us into the dream team."

"Don't mention it," Slater said. He felt lower than a snake's belly, deceiving his friend this way. But even if Jessie was a severe pain in the neck most of the time, she was definitely worth it.

▲   ▼   ▲

Jessie squirmed under Slater's car. She reached for the wing nut under the oil pan. Luckily, she knew right where it was, thanks to all those Saturdays she'd spent helping Slater work on this heap of metal. This was payback.

She twisted the nut and carefully scooted back so that she wouldn't get oil on her clothes. She got snagged for a minute but pulled free. The oil began to dribble out in a trickle that quickly became a stream. In another two minutes, Slater would have no oil in his engine. He sure wouldn't get far.

Quickly, she wriggled out the rest of the way and ran back down the road. Lisa had commandeered six hefty surfers, who had simply lifted up the Toyota and carried it back to the road. She was busy thanking them and taking their phone numbers.

Jessie held up a soda bottle. "I got the sand," she told Lisa. "Let's get moving, pronto."

"What about Slater?" Lisa asked as she gave the guys a final, wistful wave.

"I took care of him," Jessie said. "He'll be lucky if he makes it back to city hall by dark." She gunned the motor and took off. "We're home free, partner. I can't wait for tonight!"

▲   ▼   ▲

That night at the country club, Kelly and Zack squeezed in behind the screen at the service area. Zack put his lips close to Kelly's ear. "Where's Brad?"

Kelly shook her head to indicate that she wasn't sure. Most of the lights in the dining room were out. Maria Elena was putting the finishing touches on the tables in the back room. She was supposed to come back to the counter and maneuver Brad so that he could be seen clearly by Kelly and Zack through the crack in the folding screen.

Zack aimed Screech's tiny video camera at the crack so that the lens was unobstructed. They had already run a practice test and discovered there was just enough light. Zack's heart was beating nervously. He'd be glad when this was over.

Just then, he heard footsteps approaching.

Zack pressed the PLAY button as Maria Elena said, "Hello, Brad."

"Are you finished?"

"All done."

In another moment, Maria Elena and Brad came into view through the lens. Zack concentrated on holding the camera steady.

"Good," Brad said. "Listen, have you thought any more about our date tonight?"

Maria Elena nodded. "I have. And I can only tell you again that I want you to stop asking me out. I think it's inappropriate since you're my boss."

"I believe in good employee relations," Brad said.

"And I didn't appreciate your threat last night," Maria Elena said.

Good work, Zack told Maria Elena in his head. Get Brad to repeat what he said.

Brad laughed. "I don't know what you're talking about."

Zack almost groaned out loud.

"What you said last night when I said I wouldn't go out with you," Maria Elena said. She sounded as though she was starting to get nervous. *Keep calm,* Zack urged her.

"You mean bumping you to the Dead Zone? We're shorthanded," Brad said. "You know that Kelly left us high and dry."

"You fired her," Maria Elena said. "After she wouldn't go out with you."

He shrugged. "So she says. But back to you and me. Are you worried that your mother won't approve of me?"

"I *know* she won't approve of you," Maria Elena said dryly.

Brad frowned. "I'd hate for her to get deported to Mexico, wouldn't you?"

"Yes," Maria Elena said. "I would. If you'll excuse me, Brad, I want to go home now."

Brad didn't move. "Are you sure? You know, things around here might be crazy next week. Wouldn't you like two busboys assigned to your station instead of one?"

"Yes, I would," Maria Elena said. "Because that's the way the dining room *should* be run. Busboys shouldn't be used for a system of rewards and punishments for the waitresses. It only hurts the customers. But if I have to go out with you to get what I deserve, I'd rather work harder."

"You deserve the best, Maria Elena," Brad said. "That's what I've been trying to tell you. Let me show you what I mean." He started to put his hands on her shoulders.

"I don't think so," Maria Elena said, pulling back and walking away.

Brad followed her for a few steps. "Wait a second."

Zack clicked off the camera. They were out of range, but he had enough on tape to hang Brad out to dry.

But the click was louder than Zack had thought it would be. He exchanged an anxious look with Kelly.

"Who's there?" Brad said. "Who's behind that screen?"

Kelly's eyes widened. Zack shrugged. What difference did it make? They had what they needed.

"It's me, Brad," Kelly said, stepping forward. "And this is my boyfriend, who you've heard so much about."

Brad frowned at them. Maria Elena looked scared. "What are you doing?" he asked. "I told you not to come around here anymore, Kelly. You're not a member of the club. I might have to call security."

"I'm a member of the club, Brad," Zack said. "Kelly is my guest." He held up the video camera. "And we just taped a very interesting conversation. You were using your position as Maria Elena's boss to get her to go out with you. If you don't leave her alone, we'll use this tape to file charges of sexual harassment against you. Oh, and you have to rehire Kelly. Did I mention that?"

Brad looked at them. Kelly stared back defiantly. Her knees were shaking, but she was learning that bravery meant going forward, no matter how scared you were.

Brad began to laugh. "You kids have got to be

kidding. You have nothing on that tape."

"Wanna bet?" Zack asked. "You can see the playback if you want."

"I didn't harass Maria Elena," Brad said. "You have nothing that would stand up in court. I told her that things might get crazy next week and she might need another busboy. Big deal."

"You said you'd stick her in the Dead Zone," Kelly said.

"Because we're shorthanded," Brad returned.

"And you admitted that you fired Kelly because she wouldn't go out with you," Maria Elena said nervously.

Brad shook his head. "No, *you* said that. Believe me, I said nothing on that tape that would be grounds for a charge of sexual harrassment. Any lawyer will tell you that. I got kicked out of law school, so I know what I'm talking about."

"Wait a second," Zack said. "You threatened Maria Elena. You said you hoped her mother wouldn't get deported."

"So?" Brad said. "I had hoped she wouldn't. She's an undocumented worker, isn't she? I was just being concerned."

Zack, Kelly, and Maria Elena exchanged glances. Brad had an answer for everything.

He laughed. "Feeling a little stupid, guys? Let's face it. Nobody's going to bring legal charges. Maria Elena can't risk it. So go back home and play in your sandbox, kids. You're tangling with the big boys. Nobody messes with Nathan Jay Porterhouse's son."

Smiling, Brad walked out of the dining room. The door shut on the sound of his harsh laughter.

Chapter 12

▲ ▼ ▲ ▼ ▲

That evening, Jessie took a long time to get ready for the ball. She wanted to look perfect when she achieved her ultimate triumph over Slater. She wore his favorite dress. It was emerald silk, and it brought out the green in her hazel eyes. She left her hair down in wild curls, the way he liked it. *Eat your heart out, sucker*, she told the mirror.

Lisa arrived to pick Jessie up. The girls had agreed last week that they'd go to the dance together and meet the boys there.

"You look hot, momma," Lisa said. Then she giggled. "I'm just trying to take Slater's place."

"Thanks," Jessie said. "Are these earrings okay? I wanted to wear my silver ones, but I lost one somewhere."

"The earrings are fabuloso," Lisa said. She twirled for Jessie. She was wearing a hot pink dress shot through with gold threads. "Do you think the photograph will pick up the gold in this dress?"

"What photograph?" Jessie asked.

"The one that the photographer from the *Palisades Gazette* is going to take, silly," Lisa said. "I hope he gets my best side. Don't you want to put your best face forward, Jess?"

Jessie laughed. "The only face I care about tonight is Slater's when he sees us accept the five-hundred-dollar check."

The ballroom at the club was already crowded when the girls arrived. Jessie spotted Slater immediately. He glowered when he saw her and stalked across the room toward her. Jessie felt a flutter of nerves. Something was wrong. She and Slater weren't getting along lately, but he looked *really* angry.

"Hi, Jessie, Lisa," Slater said. "I hope you enjoyed the ride here."

"Sure," Jessie said nervously. "What do you mean, Slater?"

"Do you know how *I* got here?" Slater asked. There was a menacing look on his face.

"How?" Jessie asked.

"I walked," Slater said. "Two miles in my best shoes. My feet are killing me. Do you know why I walked, Jessie?"

"No," Jessie said faintly.

"Because my car is dead. And do you know

why my car is dead? Because somebody drained all the oil out of it. My warning light is broken, so I burned out the engine. Do you know how much it costs to fix a burned-out engine? Six hundred dollars!"

"Gosh, Slater," Lisa said. "How do you know somebody did it? You could have had a leak."

Slater reached into his jacket pocket and withdrew a silver earring. He held it in front of Jessie's face. "I found this wedged in the car frame."

"She could have lost that anytime," Lisa said.

"Don't bother, Lisa," Jessie said. She turned to her boyfriend. "Okay, I confess. I did it, Slater. I didn't mean to put your car out of commission, though."

"Right," Slater said. "Just like you didn't mean to give me a black eye. Did you notice that it's turning purple now?"

"That's okay, Slater," Lisa assured him. "It doesn't clash with your suit."

"How was I to know that your oil light was broken?" Jessie asked. "I just wanted to slow you down. You deserved it. You—"

"Save it, Spano," Slater said disgustedly. "I've heard it all before. I'm a macho pig with the sensitivity of a cow."

"If the hoof fits," Jessie said.

"Well, I'll tell you something," Slater said in a low, dangerous voice. "I did some thinking this afternoon while I was waiting for the tow truck. Your competitiveness is just too hard to take. I need a woman who loves me, not one who just wants to score points off me. I can't live without my wheels. But I *can* live without you, Jessie. And I bet I'll be a whole lot happier." Slater walked away.

"Gee," Lisa said. "He sounded like he meant that."

Jessie tossed her head. "So? He'll get over it. How about *his* competitiveness? Don't forget how he pulled that slimy double cross on you, Lisa."

"Right," Lisa said.

Screech came up, straightening his plaid tie. "Greetings, girls. I, for one, want to tell you that I don't hold a grudge."

"Thanks, Screech," Jessie said. "Slater really took it personally."

"I didn't mean I didn't hold a grudge against *you*," Screech said. "I don't hold a grudge against *Slater*. Even though I could have won something for the first time in my life, I don't care. I guess I'm just a sucker for true love."

"True love?" Jessie asked. "What do you mean?"

Screech leaned closer. "Well, we all know who's the big, mushy romantic around here. I won't mention any names, but his initials are A. C. Slater."

"What are you talking about, Screech?" Jessie asked.

"Translation, dweeb," Lisa said.

"Slater drained the water out of his radiator so the car would overheat," Screech said. "He had to confess to me when a wrench fell out of his pocket. He told me all about the deal with you, Lisa. He sabotaged us so that we wouldn't win. Of course, it turned out he didn't have to do anything at all. The car had an oil leak, can you believe it? Bad luck. Or should I say good luck? We didn't get to city hall until after six o'clock. So I guess neither team will win after all. What time did you guys get to city hall?"

Jessie felt all the color drain from her face. Slater hadn't double-crossed Lisa after all! All this time, he'd been plotting behind her back to lose. Just because he really loved her.

"Oops," Lisa said in a small voice. "I guess we messed up big time."

"That's okay, Lisa," Screech said. "You were *supposed* to mess up, remember?"

Jessie looked up at the podium. Damon Frederick was heading to the microphone. For the first time in her life, Jessie prayed that she wouldn't come in first. Because if she won, she just might lose the most important thing in her life.

▲   ▼   ▲

Kelly stood gloomily in a small anteroom off the ballroom. She and Zack had been too bummed to join the festivities. Brad had won, after all.

"I just feel so stupid," Kelly said. "I should have thought it through more."

"Give yourself a break, Kelly," Zack said. "Brad is older and has more experience. I guess he really knows the legalities of the situation. Unless he's bluffing."

"He could be," Kelly said. "But the bottom line is, we can't go the legal route. Maria Elena is too scared."

A woman dressed in a frilly, powder blue dress ran in. "Have you seen Damon Frederick?" she asked, wringing her hands nervously.

"I think he went to the podium," Zack said.

"Oh, dear. Oh, dear," the woman said.

"Is there anything we can help you with?" Zack asked politely.

"I don't know, dears. Oh, dear. Oh, my. We should have planned this better, I guess. I'm Eloise Caldwell, of the Ladies of Palisades Beautification Committee?"

"Of course," Zack said. "I should have recognized you."

"We have a video we're going to show after they announce the winner of the scavenger hunt. It's on the history of our beautiful flowering shrubs here in Palisades. Damon is supposed to run the sound system. It's set up in back of the ballroom. But we forgot that he was announcing the winner. He'll never have time to get through the crowd to the back of the room, and it has to be timed precisely, you see. If there's a lag, the band will start playing and everyone will start dancing and no one will get to see it! And the tape is *so* educational."

"Oh, my gosh!" Zack said, standing up. "We can't let that happen. The future of every flowering shrub in Palisades is at stake."

Mrs. Caldwell beamed at him. "It's so nice to see a young man appreciate horticulture. Can you help us? You young people know about these electronic things."

"I'll be happy to help you ladies," Zack promised. He turned to Kelly. "I think I just solved our problem," he murmured.

"You did? Do I have a problem with a hydrangea bush that I don't know about?" Kelly asked.

"You were right a minute ago, Kelly," Zack said. "We can't try Brad in a normal court, but we can try him in a place that would bother Bradford Jay Porterhouse even more. The court of public opinion. What matters to Brad more than anything? His family name. His standing at the club. His *father*."

Kelly stared at him as the realization of what Zack was going to do sank in. She gasped. "You can't!"

"Remember Brad laughing at us. Remember what he said to Maria Elena. Remember what he did to you. Then give me one good reason why not," Zack said.

Kelly gave a slow grin. "What are we waiting for?" she said.

▲   ▼   ▲

"And the winners of the five-hundred-dollar check and memberships to the Palisades Historical Society are—"

Jessie closed her eyes. *Please, don't let it be me.*

"Jessie Spano and Lisa Turtle!"

Jessie and Lisa groaned.

"Come on up and get your prizes, ladies!" Damon Frederick called.

Plastering smiles on their faces, the two young women took the five-hundred-dollar check. Jessie wanted to burst into tears. Lisa was so upset, she forgot to angle her best side toward the photographer.

Jessie and Lisa thanked Mr. Frederick and then walked down the steps of the podium. They stopped.

"I feel awful," Lisa said.

Suddenly, Jessie had an idea. She whispered in Lisa's ear.

"I think it's a great idea," Lisa said approvingly. "Go for it, girl. Good luck."

Jessie ran across the ballroom. She saw Slater standing alone, and she went up to him. She held out the check.

"Lisa and I want you to have this," she said. "Consider it a down payment on fixing your car. We'll come up with the rest if you need it."

Slater just stared at the check. He didn't say a word.

"We don't feel like we deserve it, Slater," Jessie said. "We really want you to have it. That way, everybody wins."

Slater's dark eyes burned into hers. "Oh, really, Jessie?"

"Slater, I blew it," Jessie blurted. "I'm really sorry. You were right before. I *can* be too competitive sometimes. And I shouldn't be that way with the guy I'm crazy about. I think what you tried to do was really romantic."

Slater's mouth twisted. "Since when is a burned-out engine romantic?"

"There's a first time for everything," Jessie said, trying to smile, but Slater didn't smile back. Tears pooled in Jessie's eyes. "I really *am* sorry," she said. "Can you forgive me? And will you please take the check? Lisa and I will tear it up if you don't."

Slater reached out and took the check. "I'll forgive you, Jessie," he said gruffly. "I know you regret what you did. I regret some things, too. We both got carried away."

"Oh, Slater! Thank you." Jessie took a step forward, but Slater moved back. She stopped. A sick feeling was suddenly in her stomach. She'd never seen this look on Slater's face before. He didn't look furious. He looked . . . *indifferent.* As though he didn't care about her at all!

"I said I forgave you," Slater said. "And I meant it. But whether I think we should be together, I don't know. My car isn't the only thing with a burned-out engine, if you know what I mean. We're just not *good* for each other, Jessie."

"I think we are," Jessie whispered.

"Well, I'm not sure anymore," Slater said. He turned on his heels and walked off.

Tears streamed down Jessie's face as she stood and watched Slater move away through a sea of faces. *Just like in Lisa's dream*, she thought. *But if it was a prophesy, I brought it all on myself.*

▲   ▼   ▲

The sound system was a cinch to figure out. Zack pressed a button and a white screen floated down. Eloise Caldwell gave her introduction and then nodded at him. Zack pressed PLAY.

Instead of a rhododendron, Bradford Porterhouse's face swam into view. He moved closer to Maria Elena.

His voice boomed out over the ballroom. "Good. Listen, have you thought any more about our date tonight?"

Everyone in the room stopped talking and looked at the screen. There was a buzz of whispers as people recognized Brad and told their neighbors who he was.

Zack saw Brad across the room. He'd been lounging against the wall, but he popped up nervously. As the tape continued to play, Zack saw him scan the back of the room. When he saw Zack, he snarled and started toward him.

Zack stayed where he was. The room was crowded, and it would take a couple of minutes for Brad to reach him. By that time, the damage would be done.

"I believe in good employee relations," Brad said on the screen, moving closer to Maria Elena with an oily smile.

A woman in the audience gasped. Zack smiled. The scene played out, just as he and Kelly had seen it. The darkness and the slightly shaky camera only added to the sense of menace and sleaziness Brad created.

When Brad suggested to Maria Elena that she could get two busboys instead of one, the murmurs rose to a buzz.

Suddenly, from over the crowd noises, a voice bellowed, "Bradford!" It was Nathan Jay Porterhouse, who was searching the ballroom for his son.

Zack faded back as Brad reached the table. His fingers scrabbled for the STOP button. But instead, he hit PAUSE. The camera lingered on Maria Elena's frightened face. Her eyes were liquid with tears. There was no doubt that she was being intimidated. The crowd gasped. Brad stabbed the STOP button, and the screen went black.

Zack slipped his hand into Kelly's. They'd done everything they could. Now it was time to see how the scene played out.

Nathan Porterhouse reached his son as the band struck up a lively tune. Nobody danced. People just stood in groups, discussing what they'd seen and heard.

"Dad, I can explain," Brad said as Nathan came up. "I was set up."

Nathan Porterhouse's expression was like ice. "By whom?"

"By that guy Zack Morris and the waitresses," Brad babbled. "I swear, Dad. They're out to get me. The waitresses came on to me, and Zack got jealous because one of them is his girlfriend. He set this up. I swear. I don't think you should do business with his father. They're sleazy people. I mean, they just *joined* the club. It's not like they're people like us. And their son is dating a waitress. . . ." Brad's voice trailed off under his father's cold eye.

"I've got a piece of news for you, Bradford," Nathan Porterhouse said. "I've *been* a waiter. I've also been a bricklayer and a short-order cook. Maybe I should have given you that education instead of Yale. Maybe then you would have learned what integrity is."

"Dad, I was set up!" Brad whined.

"That's enough!" Nathan Porterhouse snapped. "I saw that tape. I believe my own eyes and ears. I'm going to recommend to the board of the club that you be dismissed immediately. And while I'm at it, I might recommend that Maria Elena for the job. She made sense. She'll probably rehire the waitress you fired. And by the way, I'll have you know. I have every intention of signing that deal with Mr. Morris. If he has half the enterprise his son has demonstrated, it will turn out to be the best investment I ever made."

Kelly squeezed Zack's hand. They hadn't spoiled his father's deal!

"But what am I going to do now?" Brad asked.

"That's your business, Son," Mr. Porterhouse said. "I've done more than enough for you. You're on your own."

Mr. Porterhouse walked off. Brad straightened his tie and started back into the ballroom. He waved at a crowd of people his age. A pretty girl in a white dress turned her back. The other girls turned away, too, and their escorts pretended not to see him. Brad's steps faltered. Slowly, he turned around and left the ballroom.

"We did it!" Kelly exclaimed.

"Whew," Zack said. "It was a close one, though. What should we do now?"

"How about a dance?" Kelly asked. "This *is* a ball, you know." She grinned. "That is, if you don't mind being seen with an ex-waitress."

"I can overlook it, I suppose," Zack said in a fake-snobby voice. "But isn't your dance card full, milady?"

Kelly smiled and slipped her arms around him. "Don't worry. I saved a dance for a hero."

Suddenly, Screech popped up from behind them. "Gosh, I'm sorry, Kelly. I'd love to dance with you. But the rumba just isn't my style!"